Enlightening the Listener
Contemporary North Indian Classical
Vocal Music Performance

The writings on Indian music have been mostly on theoretical aspects and mainly by theoreticians and not by practising musicians. It is still rare to find a woman performer who has written on music performance from different angles. In *Enlightening the Listener,* Prabha Atre, a noted vocalist examines with a liberal and holistic approach various aspects of a Contemporary North Indian Classical Vocal Music Performance for a lay listener. While doing this she critically and objectively tries to seek in the context of changing times new meaning appropriate to what has come down from tradition. Her academic background, analytical mind, logical approach and communication skills put this book in a special category.

This book deals with various aspects of music performance as also persons and institutions involved in 'Music Making'. Dr. Atre's diverse experience as a singer, composer, teacher and thinker has lent authenticity to this work. From a point of view of a lay listener, she unfolds artistically the creative process of music making and thus gently guides the reader towards better appreciation.

The accompanying cassette with illustrations is an added feature of this book. Listening to it will help the reader to identify the musical material and forms and gives an idea of the techniques involved.

Padmashri and Sangeet Natak Akademi awardee Dr. Prabha Atre is an eminent personality in the field of music. She is revered as a brilliant thinker, performer, academician, composer, and teacher. A former Assistant Producer with the All India Radio, former Professor and Head of the Department of Music, SNDT Women's University, Mumbai and former Producer-Director of the recording company 'Swarashree' devoted only to classical music, Dr. Prabha Atre has a rare blend of skill and insight. Dr. Atre has displayed constant innovation and creative endeavour which has distinguished her from other vocalists both in the classical and light-classical idioms.

A senior vocalist representing the Kirana *gharaanaa*, Dr. Atre was trained by the late Shri Sureshbabu Mane and Padmabhushan Hirabai Badodekar and drew inspiration from the styles of late Amir Khan and Bade Ghulam Ali Khan.

Enlightening the Listener

Contemporary North Indian Classical
Vocal Music Performance

Prabha Atre

*duo accompanying
audio-cassette with illustrations*

Munshiram Manoharlal
Publishers Pvt. Ltd.

ISBN 81-215-0940-8
First published 2000

Typeset, printed and published by
Munshiram Manoharlal Publishers Pvt. Ltd.,
Post Box 5715, 54 Rani Jhansi Road, New Delhi 110 055.

*My life
intimately linked with notes
I dedicate to thee, O Rasika!**

*The bond between us
continues
from one birth to another.
Mark this well, O Rasika!*

*In life and in death
I am entirely yours.
No separate identity!
No discernible bonds!*

Rasika = connoisseur

CONTENTS

PREFACE

I am a professional singer. I have been singing since my childhood. I was trained in the traditional 'guru-shishya paramparaa' of music education which discouraged questioning and commanded complete surrender.

I was lucky to have a *guru* who let me grow independently. My strong educational background and academic interest helped me look upon music with open eyes.

My association with All India Radio as Assistant Music Producer, with SNDT Women's University as Professor and Head of the Department of Music and with 'Swarashree' Recording Company as Producer-Director exposed me to the whole world of music inside and outside. This exposure offered a broader perspective of various aspects of music and music activity. It not only enriched my understanding and stimulated my thinking, but gave an insight which helped me in music making in terms of skill, technique, content and expression.

My need to compose, my need to communicate with my audience made me examine critically and objectively the various things that were happening in the field of music—in the actual contemporary performance.

The articles in this book sing mainly about the contemporary performance, related activities and people involved in music making directly or indirectly.

These articles are meant to be complete in themselves for independent reading. There are, therefore, repetition of some ideas. I am aware of them, but I have not edited those portions so that the reader can read these articles independently without having to refer to other articles. The reading of 'repeated portions' will also help the listener to understand the concepts better. I have arranged the articles maintaining continuity of their thematic consistency.

TECHNICAL TERMS

The technical terms that are used in Hindustani music today are given in italics and their spelling is also made according to their actual pronunciation. The diacritical marks have been dropped to avoid confusion for a lay listener.

NOTATION

I have followed generally Bhatkhande system of notation using English letters—*S, R, G, M, P, D, N* in place of Devanagari letters for notes (*swara*-s)—*Saa, Re, Ga, Ma, Pa, Dha, Ni* respectively.

NOTES

Shuddha (natural) notes—*S, R, G, M, P, D, N*
Komal (flat) notes—*r, g, d, n*
Teevra (sharp) notes—*m*

Mandra saptak (lower octave) notes
Ṣ, Ṛ, Ġ, Ṃ, Ṗ, Ḍ, Ṇ—a dot below the note

Madhya saptak (middle octave) notes
S, R, G, M, P, D, N

Taar saptak (higher octave) notes
Ṡ, Ṙ, Ġ, Ṁ, Ṗ, Ḋ, Ṅ—a dot above the note

Taal Signs

First beat—*sam*—is shown by 'X'
Silent beat—*khaali*—is shown by '0'
          taali—shown by numbers 1, 2, 3, etc.
Grouping of beats is shown by bars—| – – – – |
More than one note for a beat is shown by a bracket *S R G M*

The book is supplemented with an audio cassette which contains illustrations mentioned in the book.

Prabha Atre

Mumbai
13 September 1999

Acknowledgements

In the context of global music performing stage and increasing international interests, the need to review constantly and consciously the content of what is taught and performed and its relevance to the tradition on one hand and the changing times on the other is far more today than it was before. This need coupled with my own desire to communicate with my listeners promoted me to work on a book for a lay listener—a book with minimum use of technical terms and less theoretical and historical details.

My first love is singing; I also enjoy composing and teaching performance—they indirectly form part of singing. However, on certain occasions when I am compelled to change the medium—like talking or writing on music performance, I realise how difficult it is to convey in words all that I know about music; all that I experience when I sing.

I started working on the book long ago. But singing always got upper hand and the book got aside. It was my well-wishers who really pushed me to complete the project. Without their persistence, enthusiasm and help this book would have remained in my cup-board.

Sudhanwa Bodas, my nephew did not want his name to be mentioned. He prepared the floppy of my book which made things easy for me. I pitied him several times for his patience at the erratic behaviour and failure of the computer. He would not like me to thank him. I give him my best wishes.

I am grateful to Mr. Ravi Paranjpe, the renowed painter-illustrator for having agreed to draw illustrations at a very short notice. His illustrations have not only beautified the book but have also made its contents more meaningful and easily understandable.

I do not know when my notes joined hands with words. I am not a poetess. It is just an extension of my musical expression. I am grateful to Smt. Susheela Ambike for translating some of my poems from Marathi to English. I am aware how difficult it is to translate a musical thought from one medium to another. Smt. Ambike has captured the essence and form adding novelty and variety to the content. I also thank Mr. Chinmay Chakravarty for helping me to translate texts of *chaiti, kajari, saavani,* and *hori* in *'thumri'* article.

I thank Mr. Ajit Soman, Mr. Ramesh Sirkar, Prof. Lalita Paranjpe and my student Dr. Tazim Kassam from Canada for helping me through the script. Their suggestions have enabled me bring more clarity and precision in the material.

I would also like to thank Shri. Devendra Jain of Munshiram Manoharlal Publishers for bringing out the book beautifully within a short notice of time.

Mehfil: The Concert—A Vision Sublime

May a note [_sur_] emerge
of beauty so divine,
that the horizon opens
to reveal what lies behind.

May a phrase [_aalaap_] take shape
with an effect so bright,
that everything is gloriously bathed
in its magical light.

May a cascade of notes [_taan_]
spurt out with no restrain
and quench every thirst
like the blissful rain.

May a pattern of notes [_sargam_]
breeze out with a wavelike pace,
that would make the wind forget
its own eternal race.

May everything fall into a beat [_laya_]
swinging with natural grace
leading the conscious mind
into a peaceful recess.

May one's performance gain strength
from a rhythm [*taal*] so sublime,
that the balance that it has lent
lasts for one's lifetime.

May the relief-beat [*sam*] fall
with such a sharp emphasis,
that for merging into the Supreme,
the soul finds a basis.

May the melody [*raag*] blossom forth
in such a luxuriant manner,
that it soon touches the Limitless
with its fluttering banner.

May the song creative [*khyaal*], so romantic
stream forth with such a fervour,
that at once it becomes the Taj
on the banks of Yamuna river.

May the charming love song [*thumri*]
display moods, in colours immensely vibrant,
the arc of thy sky as it were,
the rainbow radiant.

May a lyric [*geet*] be musically rendered
in a tune with so much feeling
that going beyond the spoken word
it conveys all the meaning.

May a prayer [*bhajan*] be sung
filled with deep devotion
the great Unqualified understood
the riddle needing no solution.

May one get an audience [*shrotaa*]
attuned to harmony and unison
making Non-Duality an experience
realised in intense communion.

May the concert [*mehfil*] become
an ecstasy, sublimely divine,
rendered immensely sacred
like the inner sanctum of a shrine.

1

MUSIC MAKING

Music has been an integral part of human life and has been functioning at various levels from prayer to entertainment. In India, as in other parts of the world, music has taken man to spiritual heights, it has eased the pressure of his relentless labour, it has given expression to his emotions and creativity. It has also filled his leisure time with entertainment. It is in this area of entertainment that the listener also takes part in the creation of music indirectly, especially when there is no written music but extempore structuring having unlimited potential. In such circumstances the listener's open response plays an important role in giving shape to music.

In a live concert of Indian classical music, the presence of an initiated listener who is conversant with the concepts, material, technique and end structures, makes a lot of difference even at the level of entertainment.

Music lovers outside India today are no strangers to Indian classical music. Many distinguished musicians from India have visited foreign countries a number of times over the decades.

Indian music is now also available on cassettes, CDs, radio, TV, and internet. Nonetheless, listeners of Indian music outside India have become familiar more with the instrumental music of India. Pandit Ravi Shankar and Ustad Ali Akbar Khan have been the pioneers in introducing Indian music to foreign audiences. As a result, Indian music has often been equated with the instruments like *sitaar, sarod, tablaa,* etc.

Unfortunately, vocal music, which is the soul of Indian music and which is also the basis of instrumental music has remained comparatively in the background. This is probably due to the language barrier or different types of vocal expressions and techniques of voice production. Very few vocalists of repute have stayed outside India for a long time or visited foreign countries regularly. However, in recent times, the interest in vocal music seems to be increasing; although the number of instrumentalists paying visits abroad far exceeds that of the vocalists.

Another probable reason for this preference is the prominence of rhythm in plucked instrumental music. Rhythm has a more striking and immediate effect on a lay listener. As instruments lend themselves more readily to rhythmic treatment, the percussionist plays a very significant role in the instrumental music of India. He has several opportunities during the recital to present solo and joint rhythmic improvisations. The fast speed and obvious rhythmic display on the instruments invariably call for thrill, excitement and applause. Instrumental music is thus dominating the performing field today both in India and abroad.

It must be remembered that Indian classical music does not remain only at the level of entertainment. It is often attributed a divine origin because of its meditative nature and cannot be easily divorced from its spiritual importance. It acts as a vital force in building up the spiritual and emotional character of a person. By its nature, Indian music makes a person concentrate and meditate. This is true not only of the performer, but also of the listener.

In the West, one approach to Indian music has been through its value in *yoga* and meditation. There is, of course, a small group of serious listeners, connoisseurs and even practitioners whose approach is from a purely artistic, academic and intellectual point of view.

As a performer, I am always curious to know how people react to music. The response especially of an uninitiated Indian listener and a foreigner in particular has stimulated me to think about music from different angles.

Of all arts, music eludes comprehension. The patterns of sound and rhythm that are created do not actually represent anything in the world around us. They are abstract in nature. The inability to recognize what is taking place and being communicated through these patterns may result at times in boredom, frustration and dislike when one is exposed to 'pure' music.

In general, most listeners react to music subjectively. They interpret music in terms of the emotional intensity that they experience. Visual images, associations and words especially in vocal music play an important role in giving emotional meaning to music. However, it must be remembered that this meaning is totally different from the 'musical meaning' of music.

To understand musical meaning, one needs to take an objective approach, where the listener thinks only about the concepts, sound material, technique, patterns of tone and time, variety, expression, flow, development of the form and so on. In ideal appreciation, both objective and subjective responses are necessary.

An introduction to the contemporary performance practice in North Indian classical vocal music, in the form of a short technical discussion, will help the listener to understand and enjoy Indian music more meaningfully.

Whether classical or popular, vocal or instrumental, North or South Indian, Indian or non-Indian, the basic constituents of music—tone and time are the same all over the world. The difference in various musical cultures lies in the approach to these constituents in terms of selection of the material, its treatment, arrangement, expression and presentation of the resultant structures. That is why every culture has its own music. On one side, music is the universal language of mankind but on the other, it is very culture specific.

Indian music has followed the path of melody and rhythm. Melody is succession of single tones perceived as unity and rhythm is succession of single beats perceived as a unit. The musical system of India has evolved to near perfection in the context of melodic improvisations. In search for an ideal form to express melody and rhythm, for centuries of creative thinking and experimentation, Indian musicians were rewarded with the concepts of *raag* and *taal*. Broadly speaking, *raag* is a system of developing a melodic scheme upon a scale; while *taal* is a system of dividing musical time into a circular pattern. These two unique concepts distinguish Indian music from the music of other cultures.

The concept of *raag* makes it possible to explore the highest aspects of melody, while rhythmic structures can be explored through *taal*. These concepts have influenced the creation, progress and experience of most musical forms in Indian music.

Around the twelfth century, Indian music developed into two distinct styles—Hindustani, which is practised in the North, and Karnatak, which is practised in the South. The concepts of *raag* and *taal* are the same in both. The two systems differ again in their approach, treatment, expression and presentation of these concepts.

RAW MATERIAL

Raw material or the alphabet of Indian music is seven basic notes —*shadja, rishabh, gandhaar, madhyam, pancham, dhaivat,* and *nishaad.* The abbreviated names of the seven notes as usually pronounced in singing are *Saa, Re, Ga, Ma, Pa, Dha, Ni* corresponding to Do, Re, Mi, Fa, So, La, Ti in Western music. Of the seven notes, the first and the fifth are stable or unchanging, while the remaining five notes have a variant. The second, third, sixth, and seventh have lower or flat variants and the fourth has a higher or sharp variant.

Note-names

		$\dot{S}$	(Saa) Taar Shadja
		N	(Ni) Shuddha Nishaad
(ni)	*Komal Nishaad*	n⊣	
		D	(Dha) Shuddha Dhaivat
(dha)	*Komal Dhaivat*	d⊣	
		P	(Pa) Pancham
		⊢m	(ma) Teevra Madhyam
		M	(Ma) Shuddha Madhyam
		G	(Ga) Shuddha Gandhaar
(ga)	*Komal Gandhaar*	g⊣	
		R	(Re) Shuddha Rishabh
(re)	*Komal Rishabh*	r⊣	
		S	(Saa) Madhya Shadja

Seven basic notes and five variants together make twelve notes of the tonal ladder. This pattern of notes of the ladder repeats as one climbs up and down. The distance between the first note and the note which has double the pitch of the first note is known as *saptak* (the octave in Western music).

The vocal range usually extends to half *saptak* below the middle tonic—*Saa*—the pitch of the first note on the ladder and one-and-a-half *saptak*-s above it. Thus the music is generally created over two *saptak*-s—full middle, half lower and half upper. The basic note or tonic (*shadja*) differs with each performer according to the range of his voice or instrument. There is no fixed or absolute pitch in Indian music such as 'C' in Western music. It is, therefore, absolutely necessary to fix the pitch of the tonic—*Saa* so that other notes on the ladder get their identity.

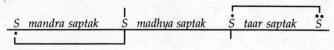

TAAL

Silence plays an important role in the perception of musical time and also in the formation of melodic and rhythmic patterns. Musical time is perceived and measured by beats which are the basic units of time. When beats are arranged in a pattern, they become 'meter' in Western music and *taal* in Indian music.

Taal is a system of dividing musical time into a circular pattern—a rhythmic cycle of a fixed number of beats whose grouping and accentuation give to it a particular character and movement. This cycle is repeated continuously during the performance to provide the rhythmic framework in which the musical form takes shape. The individual beats of the *taal* are counted by hand showing its characteristic pattern and are also played on the drums in different ways to produce various sounds. This helps one recognize the progression of the *taal* as well as the position of the individual beats within the *taal*. Various syllables such as *dhaa*, *ghe*, *tirakita*, *dhin*, *tin*, *naa*, etc., are used to identify the beats. When these syllables are grouped according to the basic structure of a *taal* they are called its '*thekaa*'.

Thekaa-s are not usually recited aloud except in solo percusssion performance. Their primary use is to identify the particular *taal* and to recognize the position of its beats when they are actually played on the drums. Drum syllables also help in composing new rhythmic patterns, in recitation and in writing them for memorising or documentation. Since it becomes monotonous to play the same *thekaa* continuously in its basic, bare form, the drummer often ornaments or decorates it by using different syllables. Therefore the musician has to develop the ability to keep track of the *taal's* progression independently of the *thekaa* variations played on the drum.

The structure of *taal* has six features.

1. It has a fixed number of beats. (*Teentaal* has 16 beats.)
2. The beats of the *taal* are grouped in a particular way. (*Teentaal* has 4 groups.)
3. The first and most accentuated beat is 'sam'.
4. The 'silent' beat is 'khaali'—the beat on which a wave is made with the hand while counting the beats of the *taal*. (Ninth beat in *Teentaal* is a silent beat.)
5. The less accentuated beat on the percussion instrument is 'taali'. While demonstrating a *taal* with the help of hands a clap is sounded on these beats. (Fifth and thirteenth beats in *Teentaal* are taali-s.)
6. It has a 'thekaa'. (*Teentaal* has three *taali*-s and one *khaali*.)

1	2	3	4	5	6	7	8
dhaa	dhin	dhin	dhaa	dhaa	dhin	dhin	dhaa
taali				taali			
X				2			
sam							

9	10	11	12	13	14	15	16
dhaa	tin	tin	taa	taa	dhin	dhin	dhaa
khaali				taali			
0				3			

All these give *taal* its personality.

Taal-s with the same number of beats and similar divisions and accentuation sound different because they have different *thekaa*-s.

Example: *Choutaal* and *Ektaal*

Choutaal: 12 beats, 6 divisions

beats —	1	2	3	4	5	6	7	8	9	10	11	12	1
thekaa —	*dhaa*	*dhaa*	*dhin*	*taa*	*kita*	*dhaa*	*dhin*	*taa*	*tita*	*kata*	*gadi*	*gana*	*dhaa*
signs —	X		0		2		0		3		4		X
hand-count —	1st *taali* clap *sam*		1st *khaali* wave		2nd *taali* clap		2nd *khaali* wave		3rd *taali* clap		4th *taali* clap		1st *taali* clap *sam*

Ektaal: 12 beats, 6 divisions

beats —	1	2	3	4	5	6	7	8	9	10	11	12	1
thekaa —	*dhin*	*dhin*	*dhage*	*tira-kita*	*tu*	*naa*	*kat*	*tin*	*dhage*	*tira-kita*	*dhi*	*naa*	*dhin*
signs —	X		0		2		0		3		4		X
hand-count —	1st *taali* clap *sam*		1st *khaali* wave		2nd *taali* clap		2nd *khaali* wave		3rd *taali* clap		4th *taali* clap		1st *taali* clap *sam*

RAAG

It is difficult to define a *raag* in words. One has to understand it by constant and conscious listening during actual performance. Its meaning and identity grow slowly within oneself. Broadly speaking, *raag* is a system of developing a melodic scheme based upon a scale in which each note is treated in a characteristic way. A scale is an arrangement of certain tones in a *saptak* in the ascending order of pitch. By selecting specific tones in a *saptak* one can obtain different scales. But before any scale can be used for a *raag*, it must satisfy the following conditions.

1. It must have a minimum of 5 notes both in its ascending and descending scale.

   Raag Bhairavi (7 notes scale)

Ascending	Descending
S r g M P d n Ṡ	Ṡ n d P M g r S

   Raag Gujari Todi (6 notes scale)

Ascending	Descending
S r g m – d N Ṡ	Ṡ N d – m g r S

   Raag Saarang (5 notes scale)

Ascending	Descending
S R – M P – n Ṡ	Ṡ n – P M – R S

2. It must have the tonic and either or both the fourth and fifth notes.

   Raag Maalkauns

   S – g M – d n Ṡ   (tonic–S, fourth–M)

   Raag Shivaranjani

   S R g – P D – Ṡ   (tonic–S, fifth–P)

3. In general, two variants of the same note should not follow immediately one after the other as in

   Raag Lalat/Lalit—two M m

   Ṇ r G M m M G, m d N Ṡ

Fulfilling these conditions, one can, by means of permutations and combinations, arrive at thousands of scales for *raag*. Although this is possible theoretically, every scale has to stand the test of aesthetic appeal, with the result that only a limited numbers are actually used as bases for *raag*-s.

How does a scale get transformed into a *raag*? Keeping in mind the rules of *raag*, the notes of the scale combine into short and long

phrases by manipulating their order, duration, accentuation, ornamentation and expression. The flexibility of North Indian music
lies in the way the *raag* rules are interpreted by different musicians.

Singing or playing a *raag* is not as easy as it may sound. It is
neither just an ascending and descending scale, nor a mathematical
permutation and combination of notes. A *raag* is just like a living
personality with its own characteristic features. That is why two
raag-s with the same scale sound different.

Example: *Raag Todi* and *raag Multaani* have—
Same scale: *S r g m P d N S*
Different notes in ascending:
Raag Todi—while ascending *pancham* is dropped
                                     S r g m – d N S
Raag Multaani—while ascending *rishabh* and *dhaivat* are dropped
                                     S – g m P – N S
Same notes in descending:
Raag Todi—descending   *S N d P m g r S*
Raag Multaani—descending   same as above

To get into the spirit of the *raag* and to bring out its features
during a performance takes years of dedicated practice and
contemplation.

IMPROVISATION

Indian music has been passed on through oral tradition. Hence,
there has been very little need for written music. The unlimited
potential of a *raag* to grow through improvisation might also have
discouraged the writing down of music. The word 'improvisation'
has to be understood in a special context. The Indian musician,
during his long hours of training and practice, thoroughly
familiarizes himself with the positions, combinations, movements
and expressions of the notes. Ranging from a single note to short
and long phrases, the combinations he practises become more and
more complex in their arrangement, movement and expression.
Thus, during performance, although he does not necessarily use
the same phrases or sequences, he is already equipped with the
skill and experience to create any variety of musical phrases.
During improvisation, he draws upon this experience. In moments
of inspiration, he often comes up with something novel and
remarkable that he has not tried before.

The first phrases in the development of the *raag* usually focus on two or three notes around the tonic, and as the development progresses, notes from the lower, middle and upper octaves are added. In improvisation, the notes of the *raag* are explored in different ways in the context of *raag-roop* or personality. However, it is the musician's aesthetic sense and his interpretation of the *raag* rules that decide whether a certain phrase is to be chosen or not.

Example: *Raag Kalyaan — aalaap*:

Raag Kalyaan drops *Saa* and *Pa* in ascending.

So instead of *S R G m P D N Ṣ*, its ascending scale becomes *Ṇ R G m D N Ṣ*.

Following this and other rules of *raag Kalyaan*, one can think of the phrases:

SṆ, ḌṆRḌS, ṃḌNSṆ, ṃNḌP, ṃḌNRḌS, ṆRG, ṆRṆG, GR, ḌṆRGRS, ṆRGmRG, ṆRṆṃG, mRGR, ṆGRS, ṆRGmDGP, PmRG, GmD, PmRG, mDN, mNDP, DmPGmRG, ṆRGmRGR, ḌṆRḌS

Ideally a *raag* has unlimited potential for improvisation. It is mainly limited by the artist's own imagination as well as outside factors such as time limit, audience response and so on. The absence of written music and the freedom to improvise within the set rules have helped the artist to introduce tremendous variety in the same *raag* structure. Therefore no two performances of the same *raag* by the same artist are identical.

RENDERING OF THE NOTES

In the formation of phrases, notes are rendered and expressed in different ways. The simplest rendering of a note is to hold it steady at the correct pitch for a long time. The ability to sustain a note, especially the upper tonic, is an admired quality in Indian music. E.g., *Saa———*Tremor in a note is regarded as unaesthetic.

The following technical terms describe the ways in which notes are usually rendered in combination:

1. *Meend*: *Meend* is a slow glide from one note to another. It is used to achieve continuity and flow while linking the notes together. Whether the glide is curved or linear, it must be smooth. Glide is indispensable in developing a melodic line.
   e.g., *Ṇ—R—G—m*

2. *Kan:* This is a grace note produced by slightly touching upon a neighbouring note from above or below or a note in between two notes. It enriches the tonal colour of main notes.

e.g.,   (N)S—main note *S, kan* note *N*

(R)S—main note *S, kan* note *R*

G (R)S—main notes *G* and *S, kan* note *R*

D (N)S—main notes *D* and *S, kan* note *N*

3. *Khatkaa:* This is produced when a note is quickly struck a second time with some force and accent.
   e.g., *mm, PP*

4. *Gamak:* A heavy shake between two notes which is repeated several times. It gives weight and dignity to a phrase.
   e.g., *mg mg mg*
   gm gm gm

5. *Aandolan:* Emphasising a note by repeatedly sliding slowly on that note from a note above or below.
   e.g., *Raag Darbaari*   *S–R–g–R–g–R–g–M–R–S*
   Raag Bhairav   *G–M–Gr–Gr–Gr–S*

6. *Murki/Harkat:* This is a cluster of notes rendered rapidly with a twist, jump and accent which usually ends on a long note. It is mainly used for ornamentation.
   e.g., *NRmPmGmPmGGR*

Each of the above has a variety of expressions depending upon the pattern of notes used and their execution.

MUSICAL MATERIAL IN VOCAL MUSIC

The material of music consists of tone and time. However, in vocal music, there is one more component—words, both with or without meaning. Tone, time and words combine themselves to form a variety of musical material.

A. *Musical Phrases*

In the formation of phrases, notes are joined basically through *meend* or glide. Other expressions such as *kan, khatkaa* and *murki* beautify the glide as required. There are four types of phrases:

1. *Aalaap:* Aalaap-s are slow musical phrases expressed mainly with vowels 'aa', 'e' and 'ee'. These are either alone or with rhythmic accompaniment. In general, the phrases have leisurely pace which can be independent of the tempo of the *taal*. However, it is common for the phrases to identify with the tempo and the structure of the *taal* while approaching *sam*—the first beat of the *taal*. Aalaap-s act as the foundation material in the development of the particular form since they help in exploring the individual notes and conveying the minute details of the form. The main and major bulk of the musical material is thus *aalaap*.

Raag Kalyaan: aalaap

	S —,	N̩ R G –,	R m – G,	m R S —,
vowel 'aa'—	aa —	aa – – –	aa – – –	aa – – —

	G m D N —,	m D N m N —,	N D P –,
	aa – – – —	aa – – – – —	aa – – –

	P m R G –,	G R S —,
	aa – – – –	aa – – —

2. *Taan:* Taan-s are sequences of notes rendered fast with vowels as in *aalaap*-s. It usually employs note-patterns in relation to the tempo and structure of the *taal*. A *taan* takes different expressions depending on the way the notes are rendered and the types of note-patterns used. They come as the final finishing strokes building up the climax at the end of the development of the form.

Raag Kalyaan: taan

	N̩ R G m D N R̈ G̈ R̈ S̈ N D P m G R S
vowel 'aa'—	aa – – – – – – – – – – – – – – – – –

G m D N S̈ N   N̩ R G m P m   D N R̈ G̈ m G̈ R̈ S   N D P m G R S
aa – – – –   aa – – – –   – – – – – – –   – – – – – – –

R̈ S̈ N D P m G R   G m D N m D N S̈   N D P m G R S
aa – – – – – –   – – – – – – –   – – – – – – –

3. *Bol*-phrases: *Bol*-s are phrases with words. They help in
   bringing variety in articulation, creating rhythmic patterns
   and lending specific emotional colour. There are five sub-
   varieties—*bol-aalaap, bol-taan, bol-upaj, bol-baant,* and *bol-banaav.*

(i) When *bol*-s enter into *aalaap*-s casually, they become *bol-
    aalaap*-s.

$$\underset{.}{N}\ R\ G\ m\ \ R\ G\ R\ \ \underset{.}{D}\ \underset{.}{S}$$

with vowel *'aa'*—   aa – – –   – – – – –
with *bol 'charana'*— cha – – – ra – – na–

(ii) When *bol*-s enter into *taan*-s, they become *bol-taan*-s.
     Taan in *sargam*—

$$\underset{.}{N}\ R\ G\ m\ D\ \overset{.}{N}\ \overset{.}{R}\ \overset{.}{G}\ \ \ \overset{.}{R}\ \overset{.}{S}\ N\ D\ \ \ \overset{.}{R}\ \overset{.}{S}\ N\ D\ \ \ P\ m\ G\ R\ S\,–$$

Taan + vowel *'aa'*—

$$\underset{.}{N}\ R\ G\ m\ D\ \overset{.}{N}\ \overset{.}{R}\ \overset{.}{G}\ \ \ \overset{.}{R}\ \overset{.}{S}\ N\ D\ \ \ \overset{.}{R}\ \overset{.}{S}\ N\ D\ \ \ P\ m\ G\ R\ S\,–$$
aa – – – – – – –   – – – –   – – – –   – – – – – –

Taan + *bol*-s   *'laago more mana'*—

$$\underset{.}{N}\ R\ G\ m\ D\ \overset{.}{N}\ \overset{.}{R}\ \overset{.}{G}\ \ \ \overset{.}{R}\ \overset{.}{S}\ N\ D\ \ \ \overset{.}{R}\ \overset{.}{S}\ N\ D\ \ \ P\ m\ G\ R\ S\,–$$
laa – – – – – – – go– – – mo– re – ma– – – na–

(iii) In *bol-upaj*, the phrases are saturated with words, to create
      a word-oriented rhythmic pattern in medium tempo.

Raag Yaman-Kalyaan
Original melodic line with *bol*-s in one rhythmic cycle of
16 beats
'Guru charana laago more mana'

S	N N̲D̲ P̲m̲ G	P – – m	GR – G M	G R̲S̲ S S
Gu	ru cha– ra– na	laa – – –	go– – mo re	ma –– na Gu
	3	X	2	0

New phrase using same *bol*-s in ¾ rhythmic cycle

G m D N	Ṡ N D P	m G R S
Gu ru cha ra	na laa go mo	re ma na Gu
X	2	0

Bol-aalaap, bol-taan, and *bol-upaj* form the material of
classical forms, while *bol-banaav* and *bol-baant* are special
to light-classical forms.

(iv) In *bol-banaav* (*bol-aalaap*), *bol*-s are placed consciously, leisurely in the characteristic phrases to convey the specific
meaning of words.

(v) In *bol-baant* (*bol-upaj*), *bol*-s are placed consciously in the
characteristic phrases to project the meaning of words,
and also to achieve rhythmic movement through words.

4. *Sargam: Sargam* are musical phrases expressed through their
abbreviated note-names or sol-fa syllables. Whereas words
give emotive colour to the phrases through their literary
meaning, the note-syllables give only musical meaning to
the phrases. Being single syllables, they are more suitable
than words for exploring novel and complex musical and
rhythmic patterns in different tempi and also for evoking an
aesthetic emotional response which is purely musical in
nature. The use of note-names also makes the listener more
conscious of the creative activity taking place.

Thus each kind of phrase—*aalaap, taan, bol*-s, and *sargam* has
its distinct quality, utility and effect in music making.

B. *Bandish*

A *bandish* is a pre-composed song, which forms a part of the
musical material used in developing a form. It incorporates the
characteristic features of *raag, taal* and form in a seed-form. It
usually has two parts—*sthaayi* and *antaraa*. Each part extends
generally to one or two rhythmic cycles. The opening phrases of
both *sthaayi* and *antaraa* are called *mukhdaa*. The *mukhdaa* extends
up to the syllable which falls on the first beat of the *taal*. *Sthaayi*
usually uses notes from the lower and middle octaves, while
antaraa uses notes from middle and upper octaves. A *bandish* can
be in slow, medium or fast tempo.

Slow tempo *bandish—badaa khyaal*

Raag Yaman-Kalyaan
Vilambit Ektaal (12 beats, 6 divisions)

Song-text

Sthaayi
Guru charana nita laabho prabho
Maangata eka hi daana tumi so prabho

Antaraa
Naada samindara ata hi kathina
Paara utaru kaise guru bina prabho

Song-text notation

Sthaayi (1 rhythmic cycle)

– Ṇ R	G m G	G m D P G R –	Ṇ R
– Gu ru cha – –		ra – – – na – –	ni ta

4

G G	Ṇ R	G M G	R S
laa bho	pra bho	– – – –	– –

X

Ṇ Ḍ Ṇ R	G – G G
Maan – ga ta	e – ka hi

0

N G R m G P	P m D N
daa – – – – –	na tu mi –

2

D m	G M	M G R –
– – – –		so – – –

0

– Ṇ	R G M	G R S
– pra bho – –		– – –

0

Antaraa (1 rhythmic cycle)

– – m	D m – m
– – Naa	da – – sa

4

D N Ṡ	Ṡ Ṡ	N N Ġ Ṙ	N m
min – – da ra	a ta – – hi –		

X

G P R	S Ṇ R
– ka thi	na Paa ra

0

G m G	P	G m G	m D N
u ta –	ru	kai – –	se – –

2

m – m	D N Ṡ	N D m G
– – gu	ru – – – – – –	

0

M M G G	R	Ṇ	R G M	G – R S
– bi – – na		pra bho – –	– – – –	

3

Sthaayi-mukhdaa
'Guru charana nita laabho' — sam falls on syllable 'laa'

Antaraa-mukhdaa
'Naada samindara' — sam falls on syllable 'min'

Fast tempo *bandish—chotaa khyaal*

Raag Yaman-Kalyaan
Drut Teentaal (16 beats, 4 divisions)

Song-text

Sthaayi
Guru charana laago more mana
Paavata saba sukha aura gyaana

Antaraa
Sata guru sangata sabase bhaari
Jyota jagaaye antarayaami

Song-text notation

Sthaayi (2 rhythmic cycles)

```
                                    S │ N   N D,  P m G
                                    Gu│ ru cha—  ra— na
                                      │ 3

 P – – m │ G R – G M │ G  RS S  N │ D  N  R  R
 laa – – –│ go – – mo re│ ma — na Paa│ –  va  –  ta
 X    2 0│ 3          │

 m m D D │ – – N Ṙ │ Ṙ Ṡ ND P m
 sa ba su kha│ – – au ra│ gyaa— — na—
 X        │ 2        │ 0
```

Antaraa (2 rhythmic cycles)

						m	m	D	D
						Sa	ta	gu	ru
						3			

Ṡ	–	Ṡ	Ṡ	D	N	Ṙ	G̣Ṙ	N	Ṙ	ṠṠ	N–	m	m	R	R
san	–	ga	ta	sa	ba	se	– –	bhaa –		– –	ri–	–	Jyo	ta	ja
X				2				0				3			

m	–	D	–	–	m	D	N	Ṙ	Ṙ	Ṡ	ND	P	m
gaa	–	ye	–	–	an	–	ta	ra	yaa –	– –		mi –	
X				2				0					

Sthaayi–mukhdaa

'*Guru charana laago*' — *sam* falls on syllable '*laa*'

Antaraa-mukhdaa

'*Sata guru sangata*' — *sam* falls on syllable '*san*'

THEMES

The text used in *bandish* covers themes ranging from the description of nature and seasons to human emotions and experiences. *Bandish*-s have devotional themes also, yet they are enjoyed more for their emotive quality, than their religious content. Although the meaning of the text is significant, as it lends emotional colour to music, its musical significance comes from its value in carrying the vocal tones through its vowels, providing variety in vocalisation and creating rhythmic patterns through its syllabic tonal structures (e.g., word '*sumira*', divided as *su + mi + ra*). The words of the composition are chosen for their musical quality and may sometimes even undergo slight changes in order to sound more musical (e.g., *baant→batariyaa*) and to meet the demands of the rhythmic structure of the composition. The languages used are mainly Braj and Hindi.

THE PROCESS OF DEVELOPING A FORM

Every form has a *bandish*—a pre-composed song. This *bandish* stands as the main pillar of the form around which the development takes place through various types of phrases. The selection of the phrases depends on the type of form. Except for the song, all music created is extempore. The selection, treatment and arrangement of the musical material gives rise to a musical form.

In the development and presentation of most of the forms, after the initial few *aalaap*-s, the *bandish* is rendered (either only the first part of the song—*sthaayi* or the full text) to establish the tempo and rhythmic cycle—*taal*. The elaboration of the form starts with improvisation usually in the middle and lower octaves. After each improvised unit the artist returns to the *mukhdaa*—the opening line of the *sthaayi*. When the development reaches the upper octave, the improvised units generally conclude at the opening line of the *antaraa*—*antaraa-mukhdaa*. Thus only the *mukhdaa* lines are repeated after each improvised unit and not the whole text during development. The sections of the improvised units of various phrases used in the development usually follow an order. First come the *aalaap*-s covering all the three octaves, then come the *bol*-s, the *sargam*, and at the end come the *taan*-s. The different sections may overlap each other; the tempo is gradually increased. An awareness of the melodic progression and rhythmic cycle is maintained throughout the improvised passage. The regular return to the opening line or *mukhdaa* contributes to creating excitement through tension and release, because a particular syllable in the line must fall emphatically on *sam*—the first beat of the cycle. It also gives a sense of completion after each phase of improvisation. The *tablaa* accompanist improvises at the appropriate time to heighten the effect of *sam*. One enjoys listening more if one watches for these moments which occur frequently in the process of development and identifies the type of phrases—*aalaap, taan, sargam,* and *bol*-s.

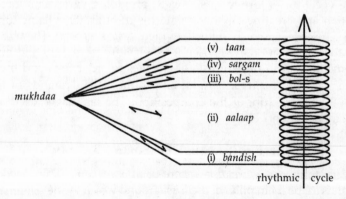

FORMS

Indian music has an antiquity of more than two thousand years. The oldest reference may be found in the musical chanting of the *Rigveda*. The singing of these hymns was restricted to certain specific occasions, such as oblations offered to Gods at sacrifices. That was sacred music, but there was also popular or profane music practised in the fields, in homes and courts which flourished side-by-side with the sacred music. Historical evidence in this respect is too scanty to permit analyses of the forms then practised.

Indian music has been preserved mainly by oral tradition from the mouth of the master to his pupil. The pillars of this oral tradition are '*guru*-s' who transferred their knowledge to their disciples. Thus they acted as a vital link between the past and the present. Their music, although not written down, continued through the ages by means of the master-pupil mode of education, assimilating features of other systems of music, which foreign rulers such as the Muslim and British brought with them. While Indian music entertained these and other influences, it did not get dispersed by them. It not only retained its individual character during the transitional period, but also enriched itself at every step by assimilating from other systems, whatever that was most suitable.

Ancient writings on Indian music speak mainly of classical music. Among the best known works on classical music we have are Bharata's *Natya Shastra* (third century BC to fifth century AD), Sharngadeva's *Sangeeta Ratnakara* (thirteenth century AD) and Bhatkhande's *Sangeeta Shastra* (early twentieth century). Although these books may form a good working aid and be valuable for reference, Indian music, it may be repeated, cannot be learnt through books alone. North Indian music is changing fast with time and it would not be correct to rely exclusively on ancient books to follow the music that is being sung or played at present.

CLASSIFICATION OF THE FORMS

To sing is a natural impulse. However, when this music passes into the hands of the intelligentsia, it takes the form of art music. Indian music encompasses a large variety, from tribal, primitive and folk to art music, which has been handed down through the oral tradition.

TRIBAL AND FOLK MUSIC

Here, music and words are born together in a natural way. There is no conscious and premeditated effort as in art music. Tribal or folk music being mostly functional in nature, it is the nature of the function which selects the words and moulds the music that accompanies it. The diverse elements in Indian culture are reflected mainly in regional, tribal and folk music.

ART MUSIC

In cities, music is used mainly for entertainment—in the form of classical, light-classical, and light music; visual music in the form of film, theatre and dance music; and popular audio/audio-visual music in the form of pop and disco music.

During its long history, Indian music has offered a large number of musical forms. Many of the forms mentioned in ancient texts on music have become extinct. Some have possibly undergone changes with the passage of time, reappearing with new names. From the earliest simple Vedic chant to the present day complex *'khyaal'* new forms have kept on emerging from the older ones to meet the demands of the changing times.

The arrangement of musical material in a particular way gives rise to a form. Each form selects its material, processes it according to its requirements and presents it to project its personality.

In vocal music words have played an important role in bringing variety in the musical material and in the formation of vocal forms. The contemporary forms in Hindustani vocal music can be classified into three categories—classical, light-classical, and light music. The relative importance of *raag* and words forms the basis of this classification.

CLASSICAL FORMS

The object of the forms in this category is to project a *raag*—which is solely a musical conception, an abstract idea. Music here exists for its own sake and words are used mainly as a means to an end. In classical forms, words tend to loose their identity in terms of their sound structure and emotional content. The forms that fall under this category are *dhrupad, dhamaar, khyaal, taraanaa, tappaa,* etc. Each form brings out different features and reveals varied beauty of the personality of a *raag*.

DHRUPAD

Dhrupad is the oldest living form after the Vedic chant. By the thirteenth century, traditional classical music had acquired this form. It flourished in the courts and temples and remained popular until the sixteenth-seventeenth centuries. With the emergence of *khyaal*, its popularity started waning and today *dhrupad* is rarely heard in music concerts. The song-text in *dhrupad* usually has four parts, namely *sthaayi, antaraa, sanchaari,* and *aabhog.* The text of the song is mostly devotional or else speaks of nature. The singing of the *bandish* is preceded by an extended *aalaap* wherein a detailed delineation of the *raag* is attempted. The *aalaap* is in three movements—slow, medium, and fast. *Aalaap* uses words such as *nom, tom* which have no specific meaning but help in creating rhythmic patterns without the drum (*pakhaawaj*) accompaniment. The *aalaap* portion includes long plain notes, *kan, khatkaa, aandolan, meend,* and *gamak*-s. Ornamentation such as *murki/harkat* is avoided. *Sargam* and *taan* are seldom found in this portion which is developed independent of *taal*.

When the song begins, the drum (*pakhaawaj*) player joins the vocalist and improvises accordingly. Henceforth, the development is made only through *bol*-phrases (*bol-upaj*), i.e., by using words of the song. Rhythmic variation through words and appropriate drum accompaniment give a stately and masculine quality to this form.

Usually *dhrupad*-s are composed in serious or heavy *raag*-s and the most common *taal* is *Choutaal* which has 12 beats. The duration of *dhrupad* varies with the artist and the audience response. It can extend from 15 minutes or less to an hour or more.

Dhrupad
Raag Kalyaan
Vilambit Choutaal (12 beats, 6 divisions/2+2+2+2+2+2=12)

Song-text

Sthaayi
Aada naada brahma naada, anahata omkaara pranava,
Jaako jogi dhyaana karata, paavata sata chidaananda

Antaraa
Hari mukhate aahata, nikasyo madhura murali naada,
Yaate akhila charaachara, paayo parama sukha aananda

Sanchaari
Udaatta aru anudaatta, swarita liye tina bheda,
Jaame pathata veda mantra, maarga reeta aahata naada

Aabhog
Taahiso sapta sura, deshee ritamo pramaana,
Prakata naama rup so,
Kharaja, Rikhabha, Gaandhaara,
Madhyama, Panchama, Dhaivata
Nikhaada shuchi vikruta bheda

Song-text notation

Sthaayi (4 rhythmic cycles)

G	–	R	N•	R	S	G	–	R	G	m	P
Aa	–	da	naa	–	da	bra	–	hma	naa	–	da
X		0		2		0		3		4	

P	D	P	m	G	R	G	P	R	N•	R	S
a	na	ha	ta	om	–	kaa	–	ra	pra	na	va
X		0		2		0		3		4	

N•	–	D	N•	R	R	G	mG	m	P	P	P
Jaa	–	ko	jo	–	gi	dhyaa	– –	na	ka	ra	ta
X		0		2		0		3		4	

m	–	D	N	P	R	G	R	–	N•	R	S
paa	–	va	ta	sa	ta	chi	daa	–	nan	–	da
X		0		2		0		3		4	

Antaraa (4 rhythmic cycles)

P	mG	P	P	N	D	Ṡ	–	–	Ṡ	–	Ṡ
Ha	ri –	mu	kha	te	–	aa	–	–	ha	–	ta
X		0		2		0		3		4	

N	N	D	N	Ṙ	Ṙ	Ṡ	Ṡ	ND	N	D	P
ni	ka	syo	ma	dhu	ra	mu	ra	li –	naa	–	da
X		0		2		0		3		4	

Ġ	–	Ṙ	N	Ṙ	Ṡ	Ṡ	N	D	N	D	P
Yaa	–	te	a	khi	la	cha	raa	–	cha	–	ra
X		0		2		0		3		4	

m	G	P	ND	D	P	P	R	G	R	–	S
paa	–	yo	pa–	ra	ma	su	kha	aa	nan	–	da
X		0		2		0		3		4	

Sanchaari (4 rhythmic cycles)

P	m	–	G	m	m	P	P	–	P	D	P
U	daa	–	tta	a	ru	a	nu	–	daa	–	tta
X		0		2		0		3		4	

m	m	D	D	N	–	Ṡ	–	_N D_	N	D	P
swa	ri	ta	li	ye	–	ti	–	_na –_	bhe	–	da
X		0		2		0		3		4	

m	N	D	P	D	P	R	G	P	R	–	S
Jaa	–	me	pa	tha	ta	ve	–	da	man	–	tra
X		0		2		0		3		4	

N	–	R	G	m	G	P	P	P	P	D	P
maa	–	rga	ree	–	ta	aa	ha	ta	naa	–	da
X		0		2		0		3		4	

Aabhog (6 rhythmic cycles)

N	–	N	N	–	D	Ṡ	–	Ṡ	Ṡ	–	Ṡ
Taa	–	hi	so	–	–	sa	–	pta	su	–	ra
X		0		2		0		3		4	

N	–	Ṙ	Ġ	Ṙ	Ṡ	Ṡ	_N D_	N	D	–	P
de	–	shee	ri	–	ta	mo	_– –_	pra	maa	–	na
X		0		2		0		3		4	

Ġ	Ṙ	Ṡ	N	D	P	R	G	R	S	–	–
Pra	ka	ta	naa	–	ma	ru	–	p	so	–	–
X		0		2		0		3		4	

S	S	S	R	R	R	G	–	–	G	–	G
Kha	ra	ja	Ri	kha	bha	Gaan	–	–	dhaa	–	ra
X		0		2		0		3		4	

m	–	m	m	P	–	P	P	D	–	D	D
Ma	–	dhya	ma	Pan	–	cha	ma	Dhai	–	va	ta
X		0		2		0		3		4	

N	N	–	N	Ṡ	N	D	P	m	G	R	S
Ni	khaa	–	da	shu	chi	vi	kru	ta	bhe	–	da
X		0		2		0		3		4	

DHAMAAR

This form is similar to *dhrupad* in presentation. However, its songs are concerned with the Holi festival, which is associated with Lord Krishna and the throwing of coloured water. It is set to *taal Dhamaar* of 14 beats. *Dhrupad* and *dhamaar* are considered more suitable for male singers because of their masculine and robust character.

Dhamaar
Raag Kalyaan
Taal Dhamaar (14 beats, 4 divisions/5+2+3+4=14)

Sóng–text

Sthaayi (3 rhythmic cycles)
Hori khelata Nandalaal,
Brija-baarana sang sohe Raadhaa pyaari

Antaraa (3 rhythmic cycles)
Mrudang dhap dhun baansuri ki dhum machi hai,
Gaavata naachata sabai dai dai taari

Sanchaari (4 rhythmic cycles)
Abira gulaal ke badara chaaye chahun aur,
Rang ki bhari hai pichakaari ata bhaari

Aabhog (3 rhythmic cycles)
Saba sakhiyana mo raajata biraajata,
Sang Saavare Raadhaa gori

KHYAAL

Khyaal is the most popular form in classical music today. Literally it means 'thought'. *Khyaal* has been widely practised since the eighteenth century. Although it is a serious form, it does not have the heavy constraints of its predecessor, *dhrupad*. Being abstract and contemplative in nature, it frees itself from the limits imposed by words and concerns itself more with the exposition of the *raag*, mainly through notes and rhythm. The words of the song-text (poem), although set to music are used mainly to enhance the total aesthetic effect which the singer has in mind.

The *khyaal* may begin with a few introductory phrases (*aalaap*) after which the *bandish*—either full song-text in the beginning or in parts according to the need—is sung. Then follows the development or unfolding of the *raag* note-by-note, phrase-by-phrase. *Aalaap*-s (*bol-aalaap*-s) in *khyaal* include long notes, *meend, kan, khatkaa, aandolan,* and *gamak.* As far as possible, *murki*-s, which are much lighter ornamentations, are avoided. After the *aalaap*-s, come *bol-upaj* and *sargam* depending on the choice of the artist, and finally *taan*-s (*bol-taan*-s). The proportion of each of these in a *khyaal* varies according to the nature of the *raag,* the singing style of the artist, his mood and the response of the audience.

There are two types of *khyaal*—*badaa* or *vilambit* and *chotaa* or *drut.* *Badaa* (big) *khyaal* is usually slow in tempo, spacious and allows for a detailed delineation of the *raag* while *chotaa* (small) *khyaal* is comparatively faster in tempo and treatment. In *badaa khyaal, aalaap*-s are prominent; while *taan*-s are the attractive feature of *chotaa khyaal.* The use of *bol*-phrases and *sargam* is left to the artist. Usually *badaa* and *chotaa khyaal* are sung successively in the same *raag,* making a single piece. *Khyaal*-s are sung in most of the *raag*-s, and common *taal*-s used are *Teentaal, Ektaal, Jhap taal, Rupak,* etc. The duration of *badaa* and *chotaa khyaal* together varies from 15 to 45 minutes or more, depending on various factors.*

CHATURANG AND TRIVAT

The forms called *chaturang* and *trivat* are basically *khyaal* presentations. They differ only in the composition of the text. *Chaturang* has four sections—meaningful words, meaningless words, *sargam* and *bol*-s used in percussion. *Trivat* has mainly percussion *bol*-s.

Chaturang (*chotaa khyaal*)
Raag Hemaavati
Drut Teentaal (16 beats, 4 divisions)

Song-text

Sthaayi

meaningless words:	*Derenaa tadim tadim tana derenaa*
	Tana derenaa tana derenaa tadre daani

*See *supra*, pp. 14 and 16 in reference to *badaa* and *chotaa khyaal*-s.

	Antaraa no. 1
meaningful words:	*Kaama krodha mada maana na mohaa*
	Lobha na chobha na raaga na drohaa
	Jinake kapata dambha nahi maayaa
	Tinake hrudaya basata raghuraayaa

	Antaraa no. 2
sargam:	*Gasaa garesaa magaresaa ninidhapamaga*
	(*g S gR S m g R S ṇ n D P m g*)
	Mapadhani saagaresaa nidhapama garesaa
	(*m P D n Ṡ g̣Ṙ Ṡ n D P m gR S*)

	Antaraa no. 3
percussion-*bol*-s:	*Taka dimi takita taka dimitaam taka*
	Dimitaam takadimitaam takadimitaam

Song-text notation

Sthaayi
meaningless words (3 rhythmic cycles)

DṠ RṠ nD PP	nDP m g g m
De- re- naa - --	ta - di - -- mta
0	3

gR SS S R	g m P D	DṠ RṠ nD PP	nDP m g g m
di-, --, mta na	de re naa –	De- re- naa - --	ta - di - -- mta
X	2	0	3

gR SS ṇ ṇ	S R g R –	– – ṇ ṇ	S S S gR
di-, --, mta na	de re- naa –	– – Ta na	de re naa ta -
X	2	0	3

S ṇ S g m	g m P D
na – de re naa	ta dre daa ni
X	2

Antaraa no. 1
meaningful words (4 rhythmic cycles)

		P D n Ṡ	Ṡ	Ṡ	–	Ṡ	Ṡ	Ṡ
		Kaa - - -	ma	kro	–	dha	ma	da
		0			3			

n D n Ṡ	Ṡ	Ṡ	Ṡ	–	Ṡ	–	n Ṡ Ṙg	Ṙ	Ṡ	Ṡ n Dn	D	P
maa -	- -	na	na	mo	–	haa –	Lo - - -	bha	na	cho - - -	bha	na
X	2						0			3		

P m gR	g m g	R	–	R	–	gR S n	S	g	g	m	m D
raa - - -	ga - na	dro	–	haa	–	Ji - na -	ke	–	ka	pa	ta dam
X	2					0			3		

D	D	n	D	n	Ṡ	Ṡ	–	D Ṡ D g Ṙ	Ṡ	n	D P g
–	bha	na	hi	maa	–	yaa	–	Ti - na -	ke –	hru	da ya ba
X	2							0		3	

R g	n D	n Ṡ	n D Pm	g R S
sa ta	ra -	ghu -	raa - - -	yaa - -
X	2			

Antaraa no. 2
sargam (1 rhythmic cycle)

g S	g R	S m	g R	S n	n D	P m	g –
Ga saa	ga re	saa ma	ga re	saa ni	ni dha	pa ma	ga –
0				3			

m P	D n	Ṡ g̈	Ṙ Ṡ	n D	P m	g R	S –
Ma pa	dha ni	saa ga	re saa	ni dha	pa ma	ga re	saa –
X				2			

Antaraa no. 3
percussion-*bol*-s (1 rhythmic cycle)

– n	D P	m D	P m	D P	n D	P m	n D
– Ta	ka di	mi ta	ki ta	ta ka	di mi	ta am	ta ka
0				3			

P m	g g	m m	g R	S S	S R	g m	P P
Di mi	ta am	ta ka	di mi	ta am	ta ka	di mi	ta am
X				2			

Trivat (*chotaa khyaal* — percussion-*bol*-s)
Raag Kalyaan
Madhyalaya Teentaal

Song-text

Sthaayi
di mi di mi gi da na ga ta ka tom dhaa gi na
dhaa ki ta ti ra ki ta dhi ra ki ta ta ka dhaa ti ra ki ta
tom tom gi da na ga dim tom tom na ga
dhi ra ki ta ta ka dhi ra ki ta ta ka dim dim dhi ra ki ta
ta ka ta ki ta ghi da na ga dhaa dhaa

Antaraa
tom tom ghi da na ga ta ka
ghi da na ga ghi daan dhaa dhaa dhaa
di gi di gi tom tom na ga gi da na ga
na ga tun di ra ki ta na ga
ta ka ta ka ga di gi na dhaa dhaa
thun thun dhaa ge ti ra ki ta ta ka dhaa
gi da na ga dhi ra na ga dhaa dhaa

GHARAANAA-S IN KHYAAL

In India, the musical tradition has mainly been maintained orally. The relation between the teacher and his pupils gave rise to musical groups resembling families. In the *Sangeeta Ratnakara*, the term 'sampradaaya' is used for the followers of the same style. When *dhrupad* came on the scene, the different styles were named '*baani*-s'. *Gharaanaa*-s emerged with the classical form *khyaal* around the mid-nineteenth century.

Gharaanaa literally means family. In the context of music, *gharaanaa* is both—membership of a particular school and a musical style. A *gharaanaa* in *khyaal* forms its style through various ways, such as, approach to or stress on melody or rhythm; cultivation and use of voice, emotional content; selection of musical material such as, *aalaap*, *taan*, *sargam*, *bol*-phrases; word-composition, its structuring and rendering; use of ornamentation, tempo, technical skill, aesthetic sense, etc. *Gharaanaa*-s are not clear-cut styles. There are differences amongst the members of the same school and today there is a lot of overlapping between the various schools. The two factors, assimilation and dissipation, bring fluctuation and variety in *gharaanaa*-s and their styles.

With the onset of commercialised mass media like radio, TV, video tapes, CDs, internet, cassettes, and books, the importance of *guru* and the oral tradition is fast diminishing. Exposure to various kinds of music simultaneously influences the individual styles. The main *gharaanaa*-s today in *khyaal* singing are Gwalior, Kirana, Agra, Jaipur, and Patiyala.

1. Gwalior is the fountainhead of all *gharaanaa*-s. It emphasises rigidity and heaviness of *dhrupad*.
2. Agra emphasizes a rhythmic and robust exposition. It is aggressive in its approach.
3. Jaipur is bold and looks for structures through melody and rhythm.
4. Kirana stresses melody, intonation and emotional content. It is sober and tender in its presentation.
5. Patiyala is intricately ornamented. It is equally at ease with melody and rhythm.

TARAANAA

The *taraanaa* is, again, a *khyaal* presentation. According to one source, *taraanaa* was originally derived from Persian poetry where the lover-beloved relationship between the devotee and God was described. Musicians who did not understand Persian took these words to have no meaning and instead explored their potential as musical syllables, to get tonal and rhythmic effects.

According to another source, *taraanaa* compositions have no literary meaning, since the choice and placement of the syllables and meaningless words depend solely upon the rhythm and note patterns. *Taraanaa* compositions thus become 'pure' musical material in vocal music and help to enhance the abstract quality of music.

There are two varieties of this form. In one kind of *taraanaa*, the treatment is exactly like that of *khyaal*. In the other, the tempo increases considerably towards the end and certain syllables and words are repeated to weave various rhythmic patterns. It then sounds like *jhaalaa* or double plucking in *sitaar* playing. A *vilambit* or slow tempo *taraanaa* is rarely heard. The duration of *taraanaa* varies according to the type, from 5 to 15 minutes or more. *Taraanaa*-s have been composed in practically all *raag*-s and *taal*-s used for *khyaal*.

Taraanaa (chotaa khyaal — meaningless words)
Raag Kalyaan
Drut Ektaal (12 beats, 6 divisions)

Song-text

Sthaayi
Ode tanana dim tadaare daani,
Tadare daani daani daani daani

Antaraa
Daare daani tadare daani,
Odere daani taadaare daani

Song-text notation

Sthaayi (2 rhythmic cycles)

PD	PP	R	G	R	S R	S S	S	R G	R
O–	de–	ta	na	na	di–	––	mta	daa–	re
0		2		0		3		4	

G	G	m	D	N R S	N	–	D	P	Pm	G R	R
daa	ni	Ta	da	re– –	daa	–	ni	daa	ni–	daa–	ni
X		0		2		0		3		4	

G	G
daa	ni
X	

Antaraa (3 rhythmic cycles)

m D	N S	N D	P	m P	m G	m	D	N S	S	–	S
Daa–	––	re–	daa	––	ni–	ta	da	re–	daa	–	ni
X		0		2		0		3		4	

G	G	G	G	–	G	m D	N R	R S	N D	Pm	G R
O	de	re	daa	–	ni	taa–	––	daa–	––	re–	––
X		0		2		0		3		4	

S	G
daa	ni
X	

TAPPAA

Tappaa is a type of *chotaa khyaal*. This form is developed only through a conscious and extensive use of typical *taan* (*bol-taan*) patterns woven through words and syllables. Words are not used for their meaning but for their tonal structure. There is no scope for a detailed elaboration of the *raag,* since slow phrases and long sustained notes are avoided in this form. Every improvised *taan* grows in size, as far as possible without resting on any note or breaking the phrase, till it joins the *mukhdaa* to arrive on the first beat—*sam.*

The text is mostly in Punjabi language and usually set to *Punjaabi taal* of 16 beats. *Tappaa*-s are usually composed in light *raag*-s. *Raag* rules are not strictly followed and notes not in the *raag* scale are often included. Since this form has little scope for elaboration, its duration does not normally exceed 10 minutes.

Tappaa
Raag Kalyaan
Taal Pashto (7 beats, 3 divisions/3+2+2=7)

Song-text

Sthaayi
Are o mendi aakhadi
Khatakadi rendi sonaa ve miyaa

Antaraa
Hoi rayaa mai makha mura mura
Naina vicha basendi tasavira
Teri shonaa me

Song-text notation

Sthaayi

P	P	DPm	GmPD	NNNDN	D	P	PDPP	m	G
A	re	o – –	– – – –	– – – – –	men	di	aa – – –	kha	di

X

R	G	R	G GR SR Gm GRS	–	N	D	P S	GGR S R
Kha	ta	ka	di – – – – – – – –	–	– ren	di so	naa– – – –

m m m G m   N N N D N Ṙ   Ṡ N P

⌞─ ─ ─ ─⌟ ⌞─ ─ ─ ─ ─⌟   *ve mi yaa*

Antaraa

P Ṡ─ ─   N D N Ṡ   Ṙ Ṡ   ⌞N N N D N Ṙ⌟   N   Ṙ ṠN
Ho i─ ─   ─ ─ ─ ─   ra yaa   mai─ ─ ─ ─ ─   ma   kha ─ ─
                X

P m R ─   ⌞N N N D N⌟   S   P D P P   P   D N Ṡ Ṡ
mu ra mu ra   Nai─ ─ ─ na   vi   cha ─ ─ ─   ba   se ─ ─ ndi

N R Ṡ N   P m   R Ṡ   ⌞G G R S R G⌟
ta sa ─ ─   vi ─   ra Te   ri ─ ─ ─ ─ ─

⌞G̈ Ṙ G̈Ṙ   Ṡ N D P m G R S⌟   Ṇ R S
sho─ ─ ─ naa─ ─ ─ ─ ─ ─ ─   ─ ─ me

LIGHT CLASSICAL FORMS

In this category, *raag* and words have equal importance; they complement each other while still retaining their individuality. Words become important because they are there to lend a specific emotional colour to the phrases, and they stretch in a beautiful way, retaining their emotional content, to suit the phrases, which characterize the *raag* and form.

Development is achieved through *bol*-phrases which include plain notes, *kan*, *meend* and ornamentation—*khatkaa* and *murki*. *Gamak*-s are avoided. *Bol*-phrases in *thumri* are of two types—*bol-baant* and *bol-banaav*. Since words are important, care is taken that they are not distorted during musical phrasing and that they retain their literary meaning. After completing the development around the first line of *sthaayi* and *antaraa*, the original *taal*, say, *Deepchandi/Daadraa* is usually changed to *Keherwaa* of 8 beats with a comparatively faster tempo. The opening line of the *sthaayi* is thereafter woven into a variety of melodic patterns in relation to the *taal* and tempo. Occasionally, *sargam* and *taan*-s are used at the end, to heighten the effect.

Although the forms in this category are broadly rooted in a particular *raag, raag* rules are not strictly followed and it is common to find notes prohibited in the *raag* being used to enhance the emotional and aesthetic effect. The word *'mishra'* is often prefixed to the name of the *raag* to make room for the use of notes not in the *raag* scale. Although the practice is to use lighter *raag*-s, there is a noticeable shift these days from lighter to heavier *raag*-s in terms of compositions and elaboration of the form. It is the treatment which makes the *raag* heavy or light. The common *taal*-s are *Deepchandi* (14 or 16 beats), *Keherwaa* (8 beats), and *Daadraa* (6 beats). *'Bandish ki thumri'* in *Teentaal* is disappearing fast.

THUMRI AND DAADRAA

The two basic forms in the light classical category are *thumri* and *daadraa*. There is a lot of confusion about what is *thumri* and what is *daadraa*, because apart from the tempo, both the forms use the same *raag*-s and the same *taal*-s, project similar themes and even use the same melodic phrases and expressions in the text elaboration. *Thumri* is slow while *daadraa* has a lilting rhythm.

The tempo influences the structure of the text composition and the movement of the phrases in the elaboration. The difference between *thumri* and *daadraa* is exactly like the difference between *vilambit* (*badaa*) and *drut* (*chotaa*) *khyaal*—a difference of tempo.

The themes used in this category are extremely feminine in nature, very often romantic and are based on the divine love between Lord Krishna and his consort Radha.

Thumri
Raag Mishra-Tilang
Taal Deepchandi (14 beats, 4 divisions/3+4+3+4 =14)

Song-text

Sthaayi
Mori eka hun na maani
Kaanhaa karata manamaani

Antaraa
Paniyaa bharana mai Jamunaa gayi thi
Bainyaa pakari mori karata naadaani

Song-text notation

Sthaayi (1 rhythmic cycle)

G MPNṠN	N N	Ṡ NnNṠ	N Ṡ
Mo - - - - ri	e ka	hun - - - -	na maa
	2		

NṠnPMG	RPMMG	R ṇ S	G M	P N R Ṡ	n PMG	M G g
- - - - - -	- - - - -	- ni -	Kaa -	nha - ka -	ra - ta -	ma na -
0			**3**			

G	g GMG	RGRS S
maa	- - - -	- - - - ni
X		

Antaraa (1 rhythmic cycle)

- - G M	P nMP	- N
- - Pa ni	yaa - - -	- bha
3		

Ṡ Ṡ Ṡ N Ṡ	n PMG	MP P	M M MMM MDnṠ	nPMG	GG
ra na mai Ja mu naa - - -	ga yi thi		Bain yaa pa ka ri	mo - - -	ri - - -	ka ra
X			**2**		

G g GM	G RG	G RS
ta naa - -	daa - -	ni - -
0		

Daadraa
Raag Mishra-Tilang
Taal Daadraa (6 beats, 2 divisions/3+3=6)

Song-text

Sthaayi
Chailavaa ne jadoo kiyo,
Nindiyaa mori le ke gayo

Antaraa

Mithi mithi batiyaa karata,
Pakari mori bainyaa hasata
Kaise kahun mai laaja aavata

Song-text notation

Sthaayi (4 rhythmic cycles)

P Ṡ N Ṙ Ṡ	n P – M G	M – P	P P n M P
Chai – – la –	vaa – – ne –	jaa – doo	ki yo – – –
X	0	X	0

G M D P M	G R G R S	S G – M P	P D n D P M
Nin di – – yaa	mo – – – ri	le – – ke –	ga yo – – – –
X	0	X	0

Antaraa (6 rhythmic cycles)

G – M	P n M P	N Ṡ N	Ṡ Ṡ Ṡ
Mi – thi	mi – – thi	ba ti yaa	ka ra ta
X	0	X	0

P N N	Ṡ – Ṡ	P N Ṡ Ṙ Ṡ	n M P
Pa ka ri	mo – ri	bain – – – yaa	ha sa ta
X	0	X	0

G M D P M	G R G R S	S G – M P	P D n D D P M
Kai – – – se	ka – hun – mai	laa – – ja –	aa va – – ta – –
X	0	X	0

OTHER VARIETIES UNDER THUMRI-DAADRA

Thumri and *daadraa* have a strong affinity with folk music in terms of themes, word content and expression. Therefore, many folk songs have been adapted for the *thumri-daadraa* style and, according to the theme, they are named as *chaiti, kajari, saavani, jhulaa, hori,* etc. *Chaiti* is sung in the month of *Chait, saavani* in the month of *Saavan. Jhulaa* describes a swing. *Kajari* sings of rains and *hori* of the spring festival of the sprinkling of coloured water.

Chaiti (daadraa)
Raag Maanj-Khamaaj
Taal drut Deepchandi

Song-text

Sthaayi
Chaitara maase saba mila gaaye
Jhulaa jhulata ho raamaa

Antaraa no. 1
Koyala gaaye chaitara sur me
Chaitara geet ho raamaa

Antaraa no. 2
Chaitara ranga me chaitara gandha me
Tana mana naachata ho raamaa

Song-text meaning

In the month of *Chaitar* (the advent of spring)
all join in the joyous singing
and the *jhulaa* swings spiritedly.

Koyal coos the *chaitar* tune,
the *chaitar* notes.

The *chaitar* mood all pervading
in all its colours, fragrance;
mind and body dancing in unison.

Kajari (thumri)
Raag Mishra-Des
Taal vilambit Deepchandi

Song-text

Sthaayi
Mehaa barase barase nainaa
Aai ri ritu barakhaa

Antaraa
Birahaa ki agni chamakat bijuri
Aavo ji sainyaa laago garavaa

Song-text meaning

Laden clouds give away
 and my eyes pour down.
The monsoon has arrived.

Pain of seperation burns like a lightening strike
O' my beloved, come, and hold me close.

Saavani/jhulaa (daadraa)
Raag Mishra-Gaaraa-Malhaar
Taal drut Deepchandi

Song-text

Sthaayi
Aayi ritu Saavna ki
Piyaa ghara naahi
Jhulaa jhule ambuwa ri
Mana moraa dukhiyaari
Piyaa ghara naahi

Antaraa no. 1
Kaise daaru kajaraa ri
Kaise baandhu gajaraa ri
Raat naahi nindiyaa ri
Piyaa ghara naahi

Antaraa no. 2
Gheri aayi badaraa ri
Bijuriyaa chamake ri
Kaise dharu dhiraja ri
Piyaa ghara naahi

Song-text meaning

It is *Saavan ritu* (rainy season)
 and my beloved is away.

The *jhulaa* swings fiercely in the mango tree.
My mind is in gloom, he is away from home.

What if I put *kajaraa* (black paste) in my eyes,
   tie flowers in my hair, doesn't matter any more.
The night is so long, he is away from home.

Black clouds gather, thunder and lightning;
   patience flies past me, he is away from home.

Hori (daadraa)
Raag Mishra-Gaaraa
Taal drut Keherwaa

Song-text

Sthaayi
Rang daar gayo mope Saavariyaa
Mori chunari bhigo di ri kesariyaa

Antaraa no. 1
Mai to gayi thi Jamunaa bharana paniyaa
Kaanhaa thaado leke pichakaariyaa

Antaraa no. 2
Mai to haari binati karata chaliyaa
Kaanhaa mane naa mori eka hun batiyaa

Song-text meaning

Saavariya (Krishna) has sprayed
   coloured water on me
   and my wet *saari*
   has taken saffron hue.

I had gone to river Jamuna
   only to fetch water
   and Kaanha stood there
   with a sprayer indeed.

After all my requests, I had but to give in
   Kaanha was in no mood to listen.

LIGHT FORMS

These forms are word-oriented and the presence of a *raag* is incidental
or accidental. The object is to project the words and their emotional
content vividly and colourfully with the help of music. Music exists

here for the sake of words. The words being of primary importance, their pronunciation, punctuation and emotional content are given utmost consideration. Music takes a secondary place and comes behind the words in import. It merges with the word structure and loses its own meaning. The tune of the song may or may not be based on any *raag*. It is common to find shades of different *raag*-s used according to the needs of the emotional content of the words.

In the classical and light classical categories, the precomposed song or tune forms part of the building material and elaboration through characteristic phrases is essential to complete the form. However, in the light category, the song itself is the total form and it may or may not be further elaborated through phrases.

The light forms *bhajan*, *geet*, *ghazal* are named according to the theme and design or structure of the song-text. *Bhajan*-s are devotional songs while *geet*-s and *ghazal*-s cover a wide range of emotions. Their poetry, which develops a certain theme, is usually of considerable length.

The forms in this category freely draw from the whole range of classical to folk music, not only in the setting of the text to music, but also in the elaboration of the form. They may be treated like *chotaa khyaal*, *thumri*, *daadraa*, folk tunes, etc., or be a mixture of all of them; the deviations from the basic scale may tend to be abrupt, obvious and quick, but they still retain their distinct musical structure because words and style dominate the presentation and musical expression. From a singer with a classical music background, these forms get a classical base and are treated accordingly.

These are the contemporary musical forms in North Indian vocal art music. Since the boundary lines between these forms are not rigid and there is much overlapping, it needs a trained ear to distinguish one from the other. The voice production as well as the combination of notes and their expression change according to the form.

ORDER OF PRESENTATION OF THE FORMS IN A CONCERT

There is an order in which these forms are usually presented in a concert.

- First comes an elaborate *khyaal* comprising both *vilambit* (*badaa*) and *drut* (*chotaa*) *khyaal*-s,
- then again a *khyaal* or a *thumri* or *daadraa*,

- may be followed by a *bhajan*. (*Geet*, *ghazal*-s are not generally included in a classical music concert.)
- This order is generally repeated after intermission.
- The concert normally ends with a composition in *raag Bhairavi*.

A full concert usually lasts 2½ to 3 hours.

If the singer is trained in only one form—*dhrupad, khyaal, thumri,* etc., then he presents only that form giving variety in *raag* and *taal*.

VISUAL MUSIC FORMS

The object of visual music is to identify with a particular situation. The established forms of music in other categories from classical to tribal, folk when transferred to media like dance, theatre and film get affected in the process of making themselves suitable to the medium. Thus there is something typical of each medium that makes its music different from the established forms in various categories.

The influence of Western music on Indian music has given birth to Indian harmony. For this reason, although film tunes are broadly Indian in nature and distantly rooted in a *raag*, they sound alien to the traditional listeners.

INSTRUMENTAL MUSIC FORMS

In addition to vocal forms which are at times played on the instruments, instrumental music has its two distinct forms.

1. *Aalaap, jod, jhaalaa,* and *gat* expressing *raag* music.
2. *Dhun* which is a combination of light-classical and light music.

ACCOMPANYING INSTRUMENTS

Drone instrument—Taanpuraa

This unique instrument is the best symbol of the melodic growth of Indian music. It is indispensable for any classical music performance as the singer/player has to continuously refer to the tonic (*Saa*) during melodic progression to check the intervals.

Taanpuraa is a stringed instrument usually with four strings. It has a gourd at the base, which is joined to a hollow stem about four feet long, with pegs at the other end. The strings are tied to these pegs. Pieces of threads (*javaari*) are placed under the strings which lie across the bridge. When plucked, the strings vibrate with a special quality of resonance. Final and finer adjustments in pitch are made by moving the beads placed below the bridge. The strings which run over a bridge are usually tuned in the order of — *Pa, Śaa, Śaa, Saa* or *Ma, Śaa, Śaa, Saa* depending on the notes used in the scale. *Ma, Pa* and last *Saa* are of the middle octave and the two middle *Saa*-s are of the upper octave.

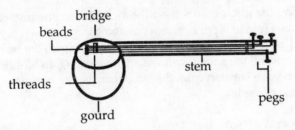

The tonic (*Saa*) is chosen according to the range of the voice or instrument and remains the same throughout the piece. When the strings are plucked continuously and gently without creating a metallic twang, they produce a drone, which lends tonal support to the performer. All music is perceived and presented against the background of this drone. Most of the female artists play *taanpuraa* themselves and sing while the male artists prefer to sing freely, and in that case *taanpuraa*-s are played by the *taanpuraa* players. There are usually two *taanpuraa*-s for accompaniment.

Rhythm instrument—tablaa

This is a set of two drums (percussion) each with a piece of skin stretched across the top. The smaller one, played by the right hand, is called the *tablaa*, while the bigger one, played with the left hand, is called the *baayaan*. The body of the *tablaa* is made of wood and that of the *baayaan* of metal, over which run leather straps, which keep the skin tops in position and serve also for varying the tension of the drum-heads. The bottom is closed. On the drumhead

a space of about 3 inches in diameter is covered with a black inky paste. The *tablaa* and *baayaan* are tuned to the tonic. Except for *dhrupad-dhammar* forms, for which another percussion instrument called *pakhaawaj* is used, *tablaa* is common for all other forms from *khyaal* to *bhajan*.

Melody instruments

Among the instruments used for melodic accompaniment, the *haarmonium* (piano type) is more common today. *Saarangi* (a bowed stringed instrument) is rarely heard. They enhance the beauty of melody and fill the gaps when the artist is resting. In addition, the artist gets vocal support from the *taanpuraa* players, who are usually his senior disciples.

THE ARTIST AND THE AUDIENCE SITTING ON THE FLOOR

Unlike in the European concert, Indian musicians, particularly from the classical field, perform sitting on a raised dais. The *tablaa* player sits on the singer's right, while the melodic accompanists sit on the left. The *taanpuraa* players sit behind the artist. The expressions on the face and body movements of most of the classical musicians in India are usually natural and not aimed at the audience. Some of the musicians even close their eyes, as if in meditation.

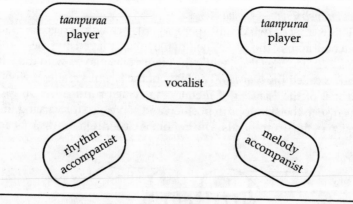

The traditional style of sitting on the floor brings the performer and the audience physically close. It results in easy give and take between the two. This rapport is very important in Indian music. It creates an intimate relationship between the performer and the audience.

Indian music concerts are not merely venues of entertainment but also workshops where music is being created and revitalised by the mutual responses of the artist and the listener. In a concert, the listener is actively involved in the performance, though indirectly. His open and conspicuous appreciation on the spot through approving words, nodding of the head and hand movements, inspires, encourages and acts as an incentive to the artist to give his best. This sort of continuous dialogue between a sensitive performer and a discerning listener has immensely influenced the development of Indian music over the centuries. It is a special feature of Indian music concerts and as a result of this interaction, Indian music continues to reshape itself.

The meditative element of Indian music demands a different attitude from the listener. It demands patience and concentration since it unfolds itself slowly, subtly like a flower.

The performing arts are live creations and are considered offerings to the Gods. Flowers and oil lamps help to create suitable atmosphere. Flowers symbolise beauty and purity while lamps represent divinity. In this atmosphere, performer and listener together embark on a voyage on the path of music which leads to the 'unknown'.

With this background of Indian music one can be in a better position to understand and enjoy a performance of Indian music. As one keeps listening consciously, one will be able to go deeper into its meaning and discipline.

INSTRUMENTAL MUSIC

Because of the melodic nature of Indian music, vocal music has been the basis for instrumental music in India. In general, instruments imitate the voice in minute details and try to produce similar expressions. Thus one finds identical sections of precomposed tune, *aalaap* and *taan*-s in instrumental music. *Bol*-phrases and *sargam* have naturally no place in instrumental music because of the absence of words. The features, typical of the instrument such as '*jod*' and fast plucking '*jhaalaa*' in *sitaar*, take on a different colour and add dimension to these phrases when used in vocal music.

In all music with words, the musical structure is basically independent of the words and that is why one can listen with pleasure to the same music played on an instrument. The association that listeners can make between a word composition and its tune on the instrument helps in the total enjoyment of instrumental music. This also plays an important role in establishing a rapport between the instrumentalist and his listeners.

Instruments

Like human voice, each instrument has its tonal quality and language that it can produce.

Indian instruments can be classified into four categories:

1. String (*tata*)	chordophones
a. Plucked	*sitaar, sarod, been, veenaa,* guitar
b. Bowed	violin, *saarangi*
c. Hammered	*santoor*
2. Wind (*sushira*)	aerophones
	baansuri (flute), *shahanaai, naagaswaram*
3. Drums (*avanaddhc*)	membranophones
	tablaa, pakhaawaj, mrudangam
4. Solid (*ghana*)	idiophones
	ghatam

Melody instruments: solo presentation

1. *Aalaap*	slow, rhythm free phrases
2. *Jod*	medium tempo rhythmic phrases
3. *Jhaalaa*	(similar to *sitaar*-plucking)
4. *Vilambit gat*	slow composition (similar to *badaa khyaal*)
5. *Drut gat*	fast composition (similar to *chotaa khyaal*)

Practically all instruments follow *sitaar* and *sarod* in presenting their musical material.

Sitaar solo presentation

Sitaar language:	This refers to different types of strokes of the plectrum—upward, downward, etc.
	e.g., *daa did did did daad daad daa*
aalaap	*nom-thom* without rhythm
jod	*nom-thom* with rhythm
todaa	short pieces, *tihaai*-s and *taan*-s in different tempos
jhaalaa	*ra da da da* (reverse)
	da ra ra ra (variations) with *tablaa*
	da ra ra/da ra/da ra ra 3/2/3
	da ra ra ra ra/da ra ra 5/3
gat	*Masitkhaani* (*vilambit*) *gat* / vocal style
	Razaakhaani (*drut*) *gat* / *taal* based style

Rhythm instruments: solo presentation

Sound produced skilfully with palm and fingers of both hands makes the alphabets of the language of these instruments.

Pakhaawaj	*thekaa*
	relaa
	paran
Tablaa	*thekaa*
	peshkaar (slow)
	kaayadaa (medium)
	relaa (fast)
	gat

Raag-Ras (Mood) and Raag-Samay (Time)

Man has used music consciously or unconsciously to express his feelings. Thus the abstract in music became concrete and specific for him. However, with the emergence of abstract or *raag* music, the musician detached music again from other things. Music existed for itself, it remained within itself. But it was not easy for everybody to approach music in its abstract state. Hence man identified melodies with seasons, and hours of the day, invoking different phases of nature through his music. He made gods preside over the melodies and sought their presence in his music. He attributed *ras*-s or moods to melodies, which helped him to create his music with distinct character. The *ras* in music can be experienced best when there is some kind of visual or verbal association to music. *Raag-maalaa* paintings and *dhyaan-mantra*-s might have helped to create a perceptible or tangible context for the *ras*-s in abstract music. The time theory also provided necessary context for *ras*.

The word '*ras*' is generally translated as emotion or mental state. Since ancient times, attempts have been made to attribute specific *ras*-s to specific melodies. Bharata in his *Natya Shastra* in the context of drama first advocated the *ras* theory in the second or third century. The theory is that when a particular stimulus generates emotions in an artist, he tries to communicate these emotions by various methods and brings out the dominant emotion to the fore.

Bharata has mentioned eight *ras*-s:

1. *Shringaara* (erotic)
2. *Karuna* (pathetic)
3. *Raudra* (furious)
4. *Veera* (valorous)
5. *Haasya* (humorous)
6. *Bhayankara* (fearful)
7. *Bibhatsa* (odious)
8. *Adbhuta* (wonderful)

Shaant (peaceful) *ras* was added by later authors.

Raag uses mainly *Shringaara, Karuna, Shaant ras*-s.

Abhinavagupta, a later commentator mentions that the highest experience of any *ras* results in *Shaant* (peaceful) *ras*. The musician's aim is to arouse a state of delight or bliss (*ananda*) in the listener, which results in *Shaant ras*.

Ras and *bhaav* (emotion) are closely related. *Bhaav* creates *ras*. *Ras* is the effect of *bhaav* upon the audience.

This was an important practical consequence of the personification of music, which thus helped the musician to distinguish between melodies having similar features.

At present, *raag-ras* and *raag-samay* have remained more due to conditioning of tradition than to be followed strictly.

The modern theory of *ras* or mood in music advocates that aesthetic emotions are generated mainly through the expressiveness of the voice, ornamentation and tempo. The verbal text, if used effectively, can also help to produce a specific *ras* or mood in music. A *raag* can express different shades of the same mood depending upon whether it is using *aalaap, taan, sargam* or *bol*-phrases. Tempo, however, plays a vital role in creating moods.

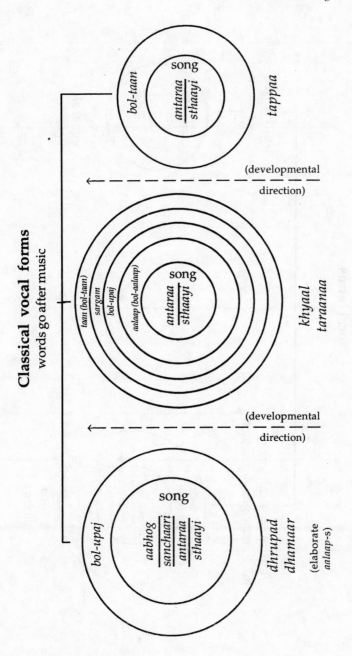

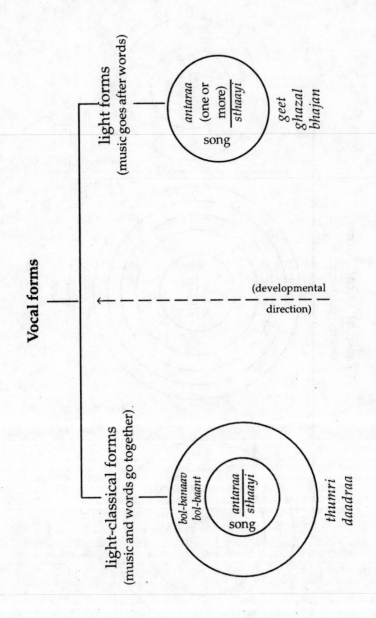

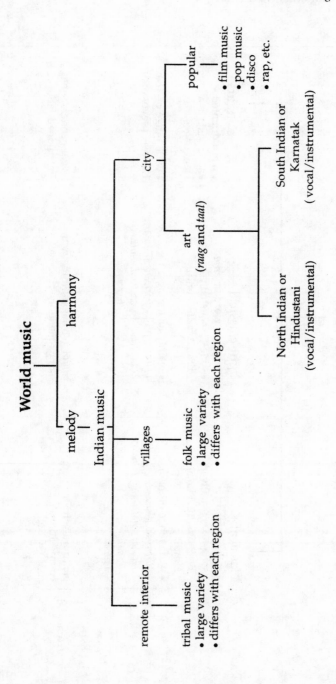

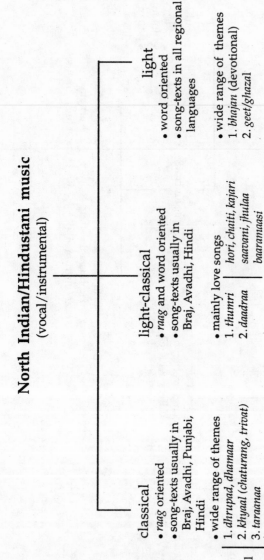

North Indian/Hindustani music
(vocal/instrumental)

vocal

classical
- *raag* oriented
- song-texts usually in Braj, Avadhi, Punjabi, Hindi
- wide range of themes
  1. *dhrupad, dhamaar*
  2. *khyaal (chaturang, trivat)*
  3. *taraanaa*
  4. *tappaa*

light-classical
- *raag* and word oriented
- song-texts usually in Braj, Avadhi, Hindi
- mainly love songs
  1. *thumri* — *hori, chaiti, kajari*
  2. *daadraa* — *saavani, jhulaa baaramaasi*

light
- word oriented
- song-texts in all regional languages
- wide range of themes
  1. *bhajan* (devotional)
  2. *geet/ghazal*

instrumental

gat (purely instrumental compositions)

dhun (strong affinity with songs mentioned above)

dhun (songs/tunes mentioned above)

HINDUSTANI AND KARNATAK MUSIC

It is believed that the Muslim invasion brought about changes in the Indian music around the thirteenth century. Haripal's *Sangeeta Sudhakara* written at the beginning of the fourteenth century mentions about the two distinct styles—North Indian and South Indian i.e., Hindustani and Karnatak respectively. Both the systems have a common basis i.e., they rest upon the concepts of *raag* and *taal*. Their difference lies in the ornamentation—the *gamak*-s, arrangement and presentation of the musical material. Therefore, if one is already acquainted with one system, it is helpful to understand and appreciate the other.

In South Indian music, most of the music is precomposed. It is therefore possible that two or more singers can sing together exactly in the same manner. The instrumental music also plays vocal compositions in their solo recitals. The audience usually knows music by heart. Only in the form 'raagam-taanam-pallavi' except for the composition, which consists usually of one line, all music presented is improvised. Musical time is kept with hand-clapping since there is no basic *thekaaa* as in North Indian music. The drum player improvises continuously on the basic structure of the *taal* i.e., number of beats and their division, and enhances the total effect.

Comparative Features in Hindustani and Karnatak Music Note-Names

Hindustani		Karnatak			
	Saa		Saa		
Komal	re	Shuddha	re		
Shuddha	Re	Chatushruti	Re	Shuddha	ga
Komal	ga	Shatshruti	re	Saadhaarana	ga
Shuddha	Ga			Antar	Ga
Shuddha	Ma	Shuddha	Ma		
Teevra	ma	Prati	ma		
	Pa		Pa		
Komal	dha	Shuddha	dha		
Shuddha	Dha	Chatushruti	Dha	Shuddha	ni
Komal	ni	Shatshruti	dha	Kaisiki	ni
Shuddha	Ni			Kaakali	Ni
	Saa		Saa		

Taal

Hindustani	Karnatak
• The number of *taal*-s is not fixed.	• Fixed number of *taala*-s on the basis of mathematics. 7 basic *taala*-s × 5 *jaati*-s × 5 *gati*-s = total 175 *taala*-s
• *Thekaa-bol*-s used for *taal* structure. Hence, hand counting not necessary.	• No *thekaa-bol*-s. Hence, hand counting necessary.
• Original tempo of the *taal* is increased several times during the performance to suit the requirements of the artist.	• Original tempo of the *taala* is not changed during the performance. The variations take place in multiples of the basic tempo.
• Particular *taal* is used for a particular form. e.g., *Deepchandi, Keherwaa* or *Daadraa taal*-s cannot be used for *khyaal* form. *Choutaal* is used only for *dhrupad*, etc.	• No such restriction.

Taala Features in Karnatak Music

Maatraa name	Sign	Number of beats
Anudruta	‿	1
Druta	0	2
Laghu	1	4
Guru	8	8
Pluta	8̇	12
Kaakapada	+	16

Seven basic *taala*-s (*Chatushra jaati* for *laghu* 4)

Taala name	Sign	Division of beats	Total beats
Eka taala	1	4	4
Roopaka taala	10	4+2	6
Jhampa taala	1‿0	4+1+2	7
Triputa taala	100	4+2+2	8
Matya taala	101	4+2+4	10
Ata taala	1100	4+4+2+2	12
Dhruva taala	1011	4+2+4+4	14

Jaati-s and *gati*-s of *taala* (for *laghu*)

Tisra	3
Chatushra	4
Khanda	5
Mishra	7
Sankeerna	9

Total *taala*-s

7 *taala*-s × 5 *jaati*-s = 35 *taala*-s
35 *taala*-s × 5 *gati*-s = 175 *taala*-s

Melodic material

Hindustani	Karnatak
• *Aalaap*	• *Aalaapanaa*

• *Bol*-phrases
   No such restriction
	• *Sangati*-s and *Neraval*
	   Sangati-s: composed melodic variations on the original song-text. The original position of words in relation to *taala* does not change.
	   Usually sung twice .

Improvised	*Neraval:* improvised

• *Sargam*
   Composed passage of *sargam* present occasionally.
	• *Chitta* and *Kalpanaa swaram*
	   Chitta swaram—composed passage of *sargam*.

Improvised *sargam*	*Kalpanaa swaram*—improvised passage of *sargam*.
• *Taan*	• Absent
• *Bandish* / song-text — flexible.	• *Saahitya* - no liberty, very rigid.

two parts ⎰ *sthaayi*
          ⎱ *antaraa*

three parts ⎰ *pallavi*
           ⎰ *anupallavi*
           ⎱ *charanam*

- Repetition of *sthaayi* and *antaraa* is left to the choice of the performer.
- Usually *mukhdaa* line is chosen for elaboration.
- *Sam* is always shown with the stress of the particular syllable in refrain.

- *Pallavi* gets repeated but *anupallavi, charanam* is sung only once.
- Any suitable line is chosen for elaboration.
- The stress of the word in refrain may not fall on the *sam*.

Forms

Dhrupad-dhamaar	*Raagam-taanam-pallavi*
• *Aalaap* without rhythm	• *Raag-aalaapanaa*
• *Aalaap* with rhythm: use of words like *ri, da, na, na.*	• *Taanam*: use of words like *aanamata, tomta*, etc., for creating a sense of rhythm.

• *Bandish:*
 	
four parts ┬— *sthaayi*
        ├— *antaraa*
        ├— *sanchaari*
        └— *aabhog*
Saahitya takes secondary position.
	• *Saahitya:*
	Pallavi (one line) - one part only e.g ., *Hare Raam Govinda Muraare maam paahi.*
	
	Although of one line, *saahitya* is important.

• *Bol*-phrases	• *Neraval*
• Absent	• *Kalpanaa swaram*
• Duration - any length	• Approximately 50 to 60 min.
• Rhythm instrument - *pakhaawaj*	• *Mrudangam*
• *Taal*-s used are *Choutaal* and *Dhamaar*	• No restrictions
▪ Song-text—refer to compositions mentioned earlier.	▪ *Saahitya* - only *pallavi* e.g., *Naayakam Vinaayakam Gananaayakam sadaa bhajaami*

Forms

Khyaal	Kriti
• Introductory few *aalaap*-s	• Few or more *aalaapanaa*-s
• *Bandish:*	• *Saahitya:*
two parts ┌ *sthaayi* └ *antaraa*	three parts ┌ *pallavi* ─ *anupallavi* └ *charanam*
• *Vilambit* + *drut* compostions	• Only one composition
• *Saahitya* secondary	• *Saahitya* important
• *Aalaap*	• Absent
• *Bol*-phrases	• *Sangati*-s and *neraval*
• *Sargam*	• *Chitta swaram* and *Kalpanaa swaram*
• *Taan*-s	• Absent
▪ Duration - any length - 10 to 30 min.	▪ Approximately 10 to 30 min.
▪ For song-text refer to *khyaal* compositions mentioned earlier.	

**Kriti*—text*
Raaga Hamsadhwani
Aadi taala
(Composer Mutthuswami Dikshitar)

Pallavi
Vaataapi Ganapatim bhajehum
Vaaranaa syamvara pradam shree

Anupallavi
Bhutaadisam sevita charanam
Bhuta bhautika prapancha bharanam
Vitaraaginam vinata yoginam
Vishvakaaranam vighnavaaranam

Charanam
Puraakumbha sambhava munivara
Prapujitam trikona madyagatam
Muraari pramukhaadyupaasitam
Mulaadhaara kshetra sthitam
Paraarichatva rivaakaatmakam
Pranava svarupa vakratundam
Nirantaram nithila chandra khandam
Nijavaamakaravi dridekshu dandam
Karaambhuja paasha bijaapuram kalushaviduram
Bhutaakaaram haraadi guruguha toshita bimbam
Hansadhvani bhushita herambham

Forms

Taraanaa	*Tillaanaa*
• Classical form	• Light-classical form
• Introductory *aalaap*-s	• Absent
• Composition: text of meaningless words, syllables	• Composition: can be a combination of meaningful and meaningless words
two parts — *sthaayi* / *antaraa*	three parts — *pallavi* / *anupallavi* / *charanam*
• Elaboration through: *aalaap*-s, *sargam* and *taan*	• No elaboration
• Fast rendering of syllables	• Absent
• Duration - Approximately 5 to 15 min.	• Approximately 5 min.
• Rhythm instrument—*tablaa*	• *Mrudangam*

Tillaanaa
Raaga Mandaari
Aadi Taala

Pallavi
Naadru drudru tomdru drudru deemtana derana
Tadare daani tadare daani tomtru daani

Anupallavi
Naadru daani tomtru daani drudru deem drudru deem
Tadare daani udana deem deem tanana
Taa kita kita taka jam taka tari kita taka jam
Taka tari kita taka tadillaana taana tir
Tadillana taana tir taka tadeem gina tom

Charanam
Meti sogasu polu neetu kulukugala poti mari ninnu
Neti pogaduchunu batikeduru chuchuchinnadira shri
Gopasaami dheeraveera venara

Forms

Thumri-daadraa	Padam-jaavali
• Introductory *aalaap*-s	• Absent
• *Bandish*:	• *Saahitya*:
two parts — sthaayi / antaraa	three parts — pallavi / anupallavi / charanam
• *Raag* and *saahitya* important	• *Saahitya* important
• Elaboration through *bol*-phrases, *bol-banaav* and *bol-baant*	• No elaboration
• Usually not composed in pure *raag*-s	• Composed in pure *raaga*-s
• Particular *taal*-s like *Deepchandi*, *Keherwaa*, *Daadraa* are used.	• No such restrictions
• Rhythm instrument - *tablaa*	• *Mrudangam*
• Duration - Approximately 7 to 15 min., or more	• Approximately 5 to 7 min.
• *Thumri* - slow tempo	• *Padam* - slow tempo
• *Daadraa* - faster tempo	• *Jaavali* - faster tempo
• Song-text mostly romantic	• Song-text mostly romantic
■ For song-text refer to *thumri-daadraa* compositions mentioned earlier.	

Jaavali
Raaga Khamaaj
Aadi taala
(Composer Dharmapuri Subbarayar)

Pallavi
Naarimani neekainadiraa jaarachora maa

Anupallavi
Dhira vinaraa shri dharamapuraadipa maa chakkni

Charanam
Botinerchinarati paatalu saiyaatale va
dhutiu sarisatila paatiyana kaadata maa

Order of Presentation of the Forms in a Concert

Hindustani	Karnatak
• *Badaa* and *chotaa khyaal*	• *Varnam*
• *Taraanaa, tappaa*	• *Kriti*-s
• *Thumri, daadraa*	• *Raagam-taanam-pallavi, Raag-maalikaa* or elaborate *kriti*
• Interval	• No Interval *Tani avartanam* (percussion solo)
• Same as before interval	• *Padam, jaavali, tillaanaa*
• *Bhairavi*	• *Mangalam*
▪ Accompanists have few opportunities for solo presentation during the performace.	▪ Lot of opportunities for the accompanists.
▪ Accompanists get secondary position.	▪ All accompanists are treated almost on the same level as the performer.

Accompanying Instruments

Hindustani	*Karnatak*
• Drone - *taanpuraa*	• Drone - *tambooraa*
• Rhythm instruments - *tablaa/ pakhaawaj*	• Rhythm instruments - *ghatam, mrudangam, kanjiraa, moorsing*
• *Thekaa-bol*-s for *taal*	• No *thekaa-bol*-s. Hence, hand counting done.
• Melody instruments - *saarangi, haarmonium,* violin	• Melody instrument - violin
▪ Melody accompaniment lags behind because of extempore presentation.	▪ Because large part of the music is precomposed, melodic and rhythmic accompaniment is identical.
▪ Accompanying melody instrument plays solo pieces only when main artist wants to rest.	▪ Practically after each vocal improvisation, accompanying melody instrument also plays solo complementary pieces of improvisation.
▪ Accompanying rhythm instrument plays solo pieces at appropriate time.	▪ Accompanying rhythm instruments improvise with vocal artist and solo melodic accompaniment continuously.

Raag-s

1. *Raag*-s having same scale and name
   Aabhogi (H)   S R g M D $\dot{S}$
   Aabhogi (K)   S R g M D $\dot{S}$

2. *Raag*-s having same scale but different names
   Maalkauns (H)   S g M d n $\dot{S}$
   Hindolam (K)   S g M d n $\dot{S}$

3. *Raag*-s having same name but different scales
   Todi (H)   S r g m d N $\dot{S}$
   Todi (K)   S r g M P d n $\dot{S}$
   [*Todi* (K) corresesponds to Hindustani *Bhairavi* scale.]

Taal-s

1. *Taal*-s having same number of beats with different names:

Hindustani	*Karnatak*
Teentaal (16 beats)	*Aadi taala* (two *aavartanam*-s of *Aadi taala* constitutes one *Teentaal*)/ *Triputa taala* (*chatushra jaati*) $1_4\, 0\, 0 = 4 + 2 + 2 = 8$
Jhap taal (10 beats)	*Roopaka taala* (*tisra jaati*) (two *aavartanam*-s of *Roopaka taala* constitutes one *Jhap taal*) $0\, 1_3 = 2 + 3 = 5$
Rupak taal (7 beats)	*Jhampa taala* (*chatushra jaati*) $1_4 \smile 0 = 4 + 1 + 2 = 7$

2. *Taal*-s having same names with different number of beats:

Hindustani	*Karnatak*
Rupak taal 3+2+2 = 7	*Roopaka taala* (*chatushra jaati*) $0\, 1_4 = 2 + 4 = 6$
Ektaal 2+2+2+2+2+2 = 12	*Eka taala* (*chatushra jaati*) $1_4 = 4$

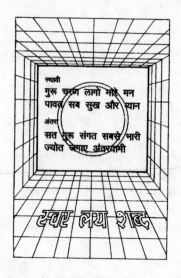

2

BANDISH: A PERSPECTIVE

Raag is an abstract concept in Indian music. It comes into being in a 'seed' form in the creator's mind and keeps growing like a mighty tree maturing through contemplation, deep reflection and its actual presentation by its creator as well as by other artists who take a liking for it. In actual presentation a *raag* gets limited by the intellect and imagination of the artist. Its infinite potential to expand and grow has made it impossible to confine it in totality, completely in any medium. Nevertheless, artists have realised that a *raag* or a genre (musical form) like *khyaal*, *thumri*, etc., can be condensed in its seed form, encased in a *'bandish'*—a small pre-composed piece.

Bandish may be broadly described as a composition confined or condensed within the elements of *swara*-s (notes) and *laya* (tempo). A *bandish* for vocal music in addition to *swara* and *laya* comprises either meaningful or nonsensical words. *Bandish*'s main function is to provide an artist with a schematic plan of a *raag* or a genre (form) constantly, and to provide him with different directions in which it could be elaborated. Artists try to elaborate the structure of a *raag* or develop a form according to their capabilities, using the framework of the *bandish* as their foundation plan.

In early days *bandish* acquired a phenomenal importance in the absence of a satisfactory musical script, notation system and printing facilities. Music is basically an auditory act perceived through the sense of hearing. Yet, there has been a continuous, conscious effort to assign symbols to notes, beats, tempo, etc., to create a kind of musical script called notation which would be helpful in writing and reading music composition. However, no notation system has so far been able to notate accurately every nuance, regarding movement and expression of vocal or instrumental music. The various ways of approaching to and leaving a note, joining two or more notes, the articulation, weightage given to grace notes, turns, modulations of the voice—there are a number of such things which are practically impossible in notation and need to be learnt by listening to actual performance only. Notation of a *bandish* represents only its bare skeleton which assists in understanding and learning only the outline of a *bandish*. A *bandish* confined in notation is dormant, inactive and lifeless. It comes alive through the voice of a singer and the fingers of an instrumentalist.

With the changing time, the 'form' of *bandish* also underwent changes to suit different musical genres, sometimes with an intention of introducing novelty, sometimes because a 'need' for change was felt. Thus, eight-parts-*bandish* in *ashtapaadi* became four-parts-*bandish* in *dhrupad-dhamaar*—*sthaayi*, *antaraa*, *sanchaari* and *aabhog*. In the *khyaal* form, *bandish* appeared with two parts—*sthaayi* and *antaraa*. Lately, especially in *vilambit* or slow pace *khyaal*, *bandish* has become generally of one part—*sthaayi*; *antaraa* getting redundant for various reasons. The *bandish* definitely represents a musical form. However, it may or may not represent a *raag*. The existence of a *raag* depends on a particular musical form.

1. In classical music or *raag* music (*khyaal*, *taraanaa*, etc.), only *raag* is important. The text of *bandish*—words with or without meaning are only a part of the musical material. A *raag* is independent of words.
2. In light-classical music or *raag*-word music (*thumri*, *daadraa*, etc.), *raag* is as important as words. *Raag* and words are interdependent and also independent of each other.
3. In light music or word music (*geet, ghazal, bhajan,* etc.), words are of primary importance. A *raag* may not be necessarily

present and even if it is there, it does not have an independent existence.

While composing a *bandish*, one has to take into consideration the specific musical form, *raag*'s position in that form and if it is vocal music, also the choice of words and their emotional content. A *bandish* becomes a *bandish* in the true sense if one is conscious of all these things. In the process of getting composed, the *bandish* also takes on a 'style' and tempo. It is very important, therefore, that one follows that style and tempo while presenting the *bandish*; otherwise the original beauty of the *bandish* is likely to be lost or affected. Most of the *gharaanaa*-s have come up with *bandish*-s of their own to bring out their aesthetic identities. Creative artists who have freed themselves from the framework of *gharaanaa* have also composed their own *bandish*-s to suit their style and have presented them in concerts as a statement of their distinct musical personality.

In Hindustani classical vocal music, with the literary aspect of the song-text slowly getting ignored for various reasons, the pronunciation of words and their emotional content also began to lose their importance. This resulted in general disregard and a lack of awareness towards the literary quality of the text of *bandish*. There also seemed less cohesiveness as regards the actual text presented. Along with the song-text, the musical structure of the *bandish* also suffered noticeably. Today, even in traditional *bandish*-s, one can notice several versions. There is no guarantee that two disciples of the same *guru* would present a *bandish* in its photocopy perfection. Some times the changes are introduced by the *guru* himself; sometimes students make changes knowingly or unknowingly. Although there is a general agreement about the structure and personality of a *raag* and *bandish*, the differences lie in details. This has made it difficult to achieve standardisation in Hindustani music.

In Karnatak music, things are different. The poetry in the song-text has some standard and general acceptance. The text being of utmost importance, the singer cannot take any liberties. This restriction has helped in preserving the text as well as its musical score. That is why hundreds of singers and instrumentalists in Karnatak music come together and present a *bandish* (*kriti*) in a choral form. It is essential in choral music that the whole piece be composed in advance to the last detail. In Western music also an individual artist cannot have freedom because of the harmonic choral nature of the composition.

Hindustani music is mainly a solo or individual performance. Therefore, in addition to extempore structuring of the *raag*, the artist can also take liberties with a pre-composed *bandish*. The advantage of this has been the emergence of immense variety within the frame—be it a *raag* or a *bandish*. Every artist can give a different perspective of the same *raag*. *Raag*'s boundaries seem to be limitless; horizons of beauty have widened. Artists have loosened the *bandish* and created more space for *raag*.

The merit of a *bandish* needs to be judged on the basis of knowledge of different musical forms and *raag*-s, command over *taal*, understanding of literature, aesthetic sense, etc. A *bandish* should not be stamped as 'good' simply because it is traditional. Neither should 'recent origin' be regarded a disqualification for a well composed *bandish*. All traditionally established *bandish*-s were 'new' at some point of time. Whether old or new, a well-composed *bandish* adds a lot of colours while developing a musical form.

Queries are often raised regarding the need for new *bandish*-s, especially when a large treasure of traditional *bandish*-s is already available for all. Music has to change with time, then is it not necessary to have *bandish*-s to represent this contemporary music? Talented artists of every period have added new *bandish*-s to the repertoire of music and connoisseurs as well as laymen have accepted and welcomed them. The number of artists composing new *bandish*-s has increased today for various reasons. The artist is liberating himself from the constraints of the *gharaanaa*. He is being constantly exposed to music of every type, from all directions. He seeks for something novel and he also desires to offer something 'new'.

New *bandish*-s that would stand the test of time would certainly be honoured as 'traditional' *bandish*-s in future years. Nothing 'new' is new in totality. It is the old which creates space for the new.

Today there is a variety of tools including notation to assist learning of music and yet there is no effective alternative to the oral tradition. The oral tradition of imparting musical education helped to preserve the *bandish*-s and the *bandish*-s in turn preserved Indian music. This is perhaps the most significant contribution by *bandish*-s to Indian music.

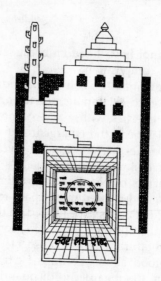

3

THE IMPORTANCE OF *BANDISH* (SONG-TEXT) AND ITS WORDS IN *KHYAAL*

Music in its purest form consists of tone and time. In vocal music, however, there is one more component—words, which form an integral part of music. In case of human beings, the production of sound is possible mainly through vowels and consonants. To make the best of this situation, vocalists have used words to their advantage:

1. Merely as carriers of notes.
2. To create variety in articulation and intonation.
3. To obtain rhythmic patterns through word structure.
4. To lend specific emotional colour.

In vocal music, words have played an important role in bringing variety in the texture of musical material.

MATERIAL IN VOCAL MUSIC

1. *Aalaap*-s are short and slow phrases sung with vowels and are usually rhythm free.
2. *Taan*-s are long and fast phrases sung with vowels and are usually rhythm bound.

3. *Bol*-phrases are phrases with *bol*-s (words) with or without rhythm.
4. *Sargam* are phrases with abbreviated note-names with or without rhythm.
5. *Bandish*—a pre-composed song-text which incorporates characteristic features of a particular form—*raag* and *taal*. It stands as the main pillar around which the development of the form takes place through various sections of phrases like *aalaap*-s, *bol*-phrases, *sargam*, and *taan*-s. Besides providing a melodic line for the accompanying *taal* structure, the part of the composition called '*mukhdaa*' acts as a reference point or resting point in the rhythmic cycle after completion of each unit of improvisation in *aalaap*, *bol*-phrases, *sargam* and *taan* sections as per the need of the form.

In olden days, *bandish*—song-text acquired importance because of the oral tradition, lack of printing facilities and absence of technical equipment like tape-recorders, CD players, etc. It was easy to remember the essential features of the *raag* through *bandish*—song-text which was a crystallised or seed form of a *raag*.

Ashtapaadi bandish of *prabandh*-s	(sung before *dhrupad-dhamaar*)	8 parts	
Dhrupad-dhamaar	(as sung earlier)	4 parts	*sthaayi, antaraa, sanchaari, aabhog*
Dhrupad-dhamaar	(as sung presently)	2 parts	*sthaayi, antaraa*
Khyaal bandish in *vilambit*	(as sung earlier)	2 parts	*sthaayi, antaraa*
Khyaal bandish in *vilambit*	(as sung presently)	1 part	*sthaayi* (one rhythmic cycle of the *taal*)

The recent trend to reduce a *bandish* especially in slow or *vilambit khyaal* to one cycle of *taal* is also an indication of the artist's endeavour to free himself from the words. One-line one-*taal*-cycle *bandish* is already in vogue in Karnatak music (*raagam-taanam-pallavi*).

Under the name of tradition, many things are accepted blindly and people don't like to part with them. Besides, the changing time also needs to be taken into consideration. The artist is heading towards free expression in *khyaal*—the only form which has the potential of beautifully representing the 'pure', 'abstract' quality of music.

The need for *antaraa*, therefore, needs to be viewed in the context of tonal structure of the *sthaayi*, the nature of the *raag*, voice range and singer's preference.

The *bandish*—song-text of a *khyaal* has two parts—*sthaayi* and *antaraa*. The purpose of *sthaayi* is generally to support the elaboration of the form in the lower and the middle octaves, while *antaraa* helps elaboration in the middle and the upper octaves.

As words cannot be avoided in vocal music which form a part of the musical material; and since, the purpose of *khyaal* is to project the *raag*, which is an abstract concept; fewer the words, freer is the artist to play with the notes. One meaningful line set to one rhythmic cycle is the smallest possible *bandish* necessary for a *badaa khyaal*. Secondly, if *sthaayi* serves the purpose of *antaraa*, the deletion of *antaraa* is the natural consequence and not a deviation from tradition.

Even in arts, survival is through necessity. For novelty's sake, one can also add *sanchaari* and *aabhog* to *khyaal bandish* or convert them to *ashtapaadi*-s. Why not?

Before one talks about tradition, the importance of *sthaayi*, *antaraa*, words of the song-text, etc., one must mull over the following points:

- Why not compose *antaraa*-s in the lower octave if the *sthaayi* is in the upper octave?
- Why not sing the whole song-text every time while coming to the '*sam*'?
- Why not give the same importance to the meaning and pronunciation of the words in the song-text of *khyaal* as in *thumri-daadraa* or light songs?
- Why are *dhrupad-dhamaar* presentations not considered incomplete when the *sanchaari* or the *aabhog* of the song-text are deleted?

It is also a known fact that in the past, many artists did not sing *antaraa* in their concerts for the fear of losing it through plagiarisation; many teachers taught only *sthaayi* to their students. Was their music incomplete? All this means that the completeness of *khyaal* does not depend on *antaraa* alone.

It is also observed that the words in *badaa khyaal* tend to lose their identity in terms of tonal structure and literary meaning, because of the slow pace of the development. In *chotaa khyaal*, since the tempo is fast, words retain their tonal structure and also convey the literary meaning naturally. Repeating one line in *chotaa khyaal* would amount to monotony. The text elaboration of the *bandish* in this case becomes a necessity.

What is important is to give due attention to the pronunciation of words and their meaning. The length of the *bandish* is immaterial if it helps in building the form and the *raag* structure. It is also logical and natural that *khyaal* uses only bare minimum of words in the song-text to bring out the 'abstract' content in the *raag* as well as the form. *Khyaal* represents music in its 'purest' form.

In instrumental music, *bandish* takes form of a *gat* having similar parts—*sthaayi* and *antaraa*. It is interesting to note that many a time instrumentalists also use only *sthaayi* to develop the form.

Astapaadi bandish of prabandh-s	Dhrupad-dhamaar		Khyaal bandish in vilambit	
	(as sung earlier)	(as sung presently)	(as sung earlier)	(as sung presently)
8 7 6 5 4 3 2 1	4 3 2 1	2 1	2 1	1

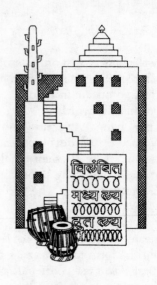

4

THE ROLE OF *TAAL* OF *BANDISH* IN *KHYAAL*

The two unique features of Indian music—*raag* and *taal* are independent structures; both can be presented without the help of the other. When they are presented together they change their roles according to whether a *raag* is to be projected or a *taal* is to be projected. They can also be complementary to each other at times.

Listening to percussion instruments like *tablaa*, *pakhaawaj*, etc., means listening to '*taal*' on these instruments. *Taal* being the main focus, melody becomes subordinate. It provides reference points to the progression of the *taal* by remaining simple and repetitive. It also makes *taal* more enjoyable.

Similarly, to listen to a *raag* is to experience *raag*'s personality, its beauty, its mood, its meaning. *Raag* being the focal point, *taal* is expected to repeat itself mainly in the *thekaa* form and provide a uniform rhythmic foundation. *Taal* is there to support melodic scheme of the *raag* and form and add to its beauty by creating possibilities of melodic and rhythmic variations. It also provides reference points as well as resting points during the development and guides the movements of the notes and helps progression.

The purpose of the classical form *khyaal* is to project *raag*'s personality, its mood and convey its musical meaning. *Taal* which enters with the *bandish* takes subordinate position. Most of the time it remains simple and repetitive.

The subtleties of a *raag* are best experienced through *aalaap*-s— slow music phrases. They allow exploration of a *raag* note-by-note. These phrases can have their own structures, movements and tempo, different from the accompanying *taal*. Therefore, to avoid continuous obstruction by the rhythmic structure of accompanying *taal*, it is kept at a comparatively slow tempo by some artists. Although in this case, musical phrases seem to float loosely on *taal* structure, they generally start identifying themselves with *taal*, as they approach 'sam'—the starting point of *taal*.

In trying to shape every phrase according to *taal* structure and its tempo, one is likely to get involved in technique only and the creative activity can easily turn into a mechanical activity. The emphasis keeps sliding from melody to rhythm and vice versa, according to the developmental requirement. In general, *taal* structure remains in the background during the *aalaap* section. However, in *bol*-phrases, *sargam* and *taan*, with the increase in tempo, the relation between tonal and rhythmic structures becomes obvious.

The usual practice of presenting more than one *bandish* of different tempos like *vilambit* (slow), *madhyalaya* (medium) and *drut* (fast) one after the other in the same *raag*, shows the need for such tempos to facilitate the movements of various kinds of phrases. At times, only one *bandish* is presented; but its tempo is increased as per the need during the performance.

Difference in various schools (the *gharaanaa*-s) apart from voice production, selection and treatment of the musical material and its presentation, can be said to be mainly due to the amount of freedom exercised from the accompanying *taal* structure of the *bandish*.

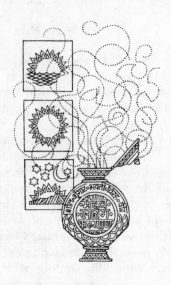

5

RAAG-RAS (MOOD) AND *RAAG-SAMAY* (TIME): A QUERY

Music is considered to be the purest form of art. Its abstract nature detaches it from all the 'known' in this world. This abstract quality of music is best represented in the concept of *raag* in Indian music. To approach *raag* in its bare form, therefore, is difficult both for an artist and a lay listener. Along with a good knowledge of the musical material and good technique the artist in the early stages looks for some outside help to transform the 'abstract' in music into the 'concrete' when he is in the process of creating a *raag*. The association with some 'known' element helps him in giving character to the *raag*. But once created, the *raag* again gets detached from the 'known' and turns to its own (basic) nature.

The word *ras* is generally translated as emotion or mental state. Since ancient times attempts have been made to attribute specific *ras* to specific melody. The *ras* in music can be experienced best when there is some kind of visual or verbal association to music.

A number of questions can arise in the context of *raag-ras* theory:

1. *Raag*-s are attributed specific *ras*-s. But very often the themes of the song-text are contradictory to the *ras*. E.g., *raag Bhairavi* is supposed to convey *Karuna* (pathos) *ras*. However, the diverse themes of the song-texts in *Bhairavi* seem to express *raag*-s inherent *ras* very effectively.

2. Quite often the themes of the song-text of *vilambit* (slow) and *drut* (fast) *khyaal*-s sung one after the other in the same *raag* are diametrically opposite.

   At times, the language of the two *khyaal*-s are different.

   At times, artists mispronounce the words, not knowing the language. However, the so called *raag-ras* does not seem to get affected.

3. Almost every *raag*, irrespective of *ras* seems to create a lively, happy atmosphere when it enters into a fast tempo.

All this goes to prove that *raag*-character, *raag*-mood are intrinsically related to its own musical material and its treatment. Its characteristic phrases and their flow give it its musical identity and beauty.

Some more points to consider:

1. Over the years, some *raag*-s have changed considerably retaining their old names. What about their *ras*?

2. What is the *ras* of *mishra raag*-s—*raag*-s evolved out of the combination of two or more *raag*-s?

3. What is the *ras* of a newly created *raag*?

4. Does an audience—Indian or non-Indian experience the same *ras* with the same intensity of a particular *raag* performance?

5. When the same *raag* is presented by different artists, does every listener experience the same *ras*?

All these queries need to be addressed scientifically.

RAAG-SAMAY (TIME)

Raag-time theory is yet another attempt to provide 'concrete' to the 'abstract' in *raag*. At one time, man was very close to nature which perhaps explains the relation between a *raag* and a particular time. Today man is far away from nature living in closed walls, in an artificial environment. His life-style and habits have changed considerably. Under these circumstances, can one relate *raag* with time?

There are various other things which make one to think about the relevance of *raag*-time theory.

1. When one listens to film songs, *naatya sangeet* (theatre songs) or devotional music based on a particular *raag*, the *raag*-time principle does not even remotely cross one's mind. On the contrary one seems to enjoy any *raag* any time.

2. Radio, TV and recording companies record any *raag* any time and that does not seem to have any effect on the presentation of the *raag*. It is only in public performances that time is imposed on a *raag* to manifest its mood.

4. One practises any *raag* any time according to his convenience and that does not seem to affect or tarnish the mood of the *raag* or its character.

5. Karnatak music is considered more tradition bound, yet it does not follow the time theory strictly. Hindustani music with all its flexibility still advocates the time theory.

6. What about *mishra raag*-s? Why should *Bhairav-Bahaar* and *Yamani-Bilaawal* be presented in the morning only? *Bahaar* and *Yaman* are night *raag*-s. Why shoudn't these *raag*-s be rendered at night also?

If we were to adhere to the time theory strictly, then there is a danger of losing *raag*-s which fall outside the concert timings. Isn't that a great loss to Indian music?

Concepts like *raag-ras* (mood), *raag-samay* (time) have been deeply embedded in our psyche due to age old traditions. They have lost their relevance, context with the passage of time, but they are still followed blindly. Don't they need to be tested scienti-fically?

It is tradition alone which provides new pathways. If tradition starts hampering the progress and growth, then it needs to be redefined in the changed context. In such circumstances, it does not get broken or mutilated, but gets rejuvenated to provide new directions.

6

Significance of *Sargam* in Hindustani Classical Vocal Music

Just as the concepts of *raag* and *taal* are unique features of Indian music, so also is the *'sargam'*, that is, singing abbreviated note-names (sol-fa names) in a performance. In other musical cultures, slow and fast phrases resembling *aalaap* and *taan* can be found, but the use of note-syllables as a regular feature in a performance is peculiar to Indian music.

At some stage of development of Indian music, the names *shadja, rishabh, gandhaar, madhyam, pancham, dhaivat,* and *nishaad* were given to its seven basic notes to identify them. The abridged version of these names—*Saa, Re, Ga, Ma, Pa, Dha, Ni* respectively is called *sargam*. For instance *Saa* is *shadja, Re* is *rishabh, Ga* is *gandhaar, Ma* is *madhyam* and so on. The word *sargam* itself is based on the first four abridged note-names *Saa, Re, Ga, Ma.* It is worthwhile asking why these note-names were abridged.

The first reason that suggests itself is quite obvious. It would be clumsy and impractical to pronounce the full name of the note while learning, teaching or practising music. As single syllables, *Saa, Re, Ga, Ma, Pa, Dha, Ni, sargam* is much easier to sing than the full note-names *shadja, rishabh, gandhaar,* etc. *Sargam* also makes it much more practical to do note-exercises and intonation exercises.

Secondly, as symbols of notation, when *sargam* syllables are sung, they help simultaneously to produce and identify a note. For example, the syllable *Pa* is used to sing the pitch *Pa*, as well as to identify that pitch as being *Pa*. The importance of this aspect of *sargam* is that it makes the activity of singing more conscious.

Thirdly, even while thinking of and composing music, *sargam* or note syllables are much easier to use and more economical than full note-names.

Fourthly, another advantage of having abridged note-names or *sargam* is that in their monosyllabic forms they help in the perception of rhythm, as well as highlight the interplay of various rhythmic permutations. *Sargam* can help in gaining familiarity with the tempo and rhythmic structure of *taal*. This is achieved by arranging *sargam* phrases in such a way that the various rhythmic divisions of the *taal* get emphasized.

Thus, in *Teentaal* of 16 beats, each beat can be sung with one, two, three or four notes depending on the tempo. The four divisions of *Teentaal* (each of four beats) i.e., the three *taali*-s and one *khaali*, can be accented by stressing on the *sargam* syllable that falls on the first beat of each division. It would be impossible to practise such rhythm oriented exercises if the full note-names *shadja, rishabh, gandhaar*, etc., were to be used, because the latter are made up of several syllables, like *sha-da-ja, ri-sha-bha*, etc. These kind of exercises also help in learning to extemporize note-patterns in various tempi that would automatically fit into the *taal* structure.

e.g., *Teentaal* (16 beats)

1	2	3	4	5	6	7	8	9	10	11	12	13	14	15	16	
S	R	G	M	P	D	N	Ṡ	Ṡ	N	D	P	M	G	R	S	
SS	RR	GG	MM													two notes a beat
or SR	GM	PD	NṠ													
SSS	RRR	GGG	MMM													three notes a beat
or SRG	MPD	NṠṠ	NDP													
SSSS	RRRR	GGGG	MMMM													four notes a beat
or SRGM	PDNṠ	ṠNDP	MGRS													

Fifthly, even while notating or analysing the structure of music, using full note-names would be very cumbersome and difficult. *Sargam* as an abridged form of these names, that is as single syllables, can perform any function much more efficiently.

Sargam, therefore, becomes essential in learning, memorising, practising, perceiving, composing, analysing, and interpreting music. Thus, we see that although the seven basic notes of Indian music were given names, they had to be abridged for practical reasons.

The question to which I now wish to address myself—can *sargam*, or the singing of note-syllables, possess any inherent aesthetic qualities that will make it valuable in performance as well? So far I have discussed the use of *sargam* in the stages of learning and practising, but what about its use as an expression of aural beauty? Before suggesting an answer, I must mention a few points about vocal music.

In vocal music, sound can be elongated (a note can be held for a long time) only through vowels. Vowels are the sounds *a, aa, i, u, e, o* which form the text/lyrics and serve as vehicles for carrying sound. Syllables are consonants prefixed to vowels, for example, M preceeding '*a*' or '*aa*' gives *Ma* or *Maa*. Words are one or more syllables meaningfully joined together.

For example,

$$guru = g + u + r + u.$$

The musical material in Hindustani vocal music comprises four kinds of phrases.

1. Slow phrases that employ vowels—*aalaap*.
2. Fast phrases that employ vowels—*taan*.
3. Phrases that employ words—*bol*-s.
4. Phrases that employ abridged note-names or note-syllables *Saa, Re, Ga, Ma, Pa, Dha, Ni*—*sargam*.

Sargam is distinct from the syllabic nature of *bol*-s, in that, the *sargam* syllables must coincide with the note position (pitch) they identify, i.e., while using the syllable *Re*, the note *Re* must be sung, or while using the syllable *Dha* the note *Dha* must be sung. The syllables in *bol*-s are not assigned any particular pitch or position.

A point to be noted is that, like *bol*-s, *sargam* uses syllables in constructing musical phrases; but unlike the former, *sargam* syllables have no literary meaning. Instead, they possess musical meaning.

In a performance of *khyaal*, the most popular form of Hindustani classical vocal music today, the development of the *raag* around the *bandish* or pre-composed song-text is usually done through *aalaap, bol-s, sargam* and finally *taan*. The form is developed through these different musical materials to weave the *raag's* musical structure around the *bandish*. It is not uncommon to find that the structure of *bol-aalaap* is often similar to or identical with that of *aalaap*. Although the same chain of notes is sung, it sounds different when only vowels are used and when words are used.

Chain of notes	$\underset{\cdot}{N}$ R G m R G R
with vowel 'aa'	aa – – – – – –
with word 'mana'	ma – – – na – –

Words have inherent rhythm due to different vowel lengths in their syllable components. For example, in the word *Saavariyaa*, the vowels are *saa—(aa), va—(a), ri—(i), yaa—(aa)*. Words also have meanings. These elements—the syllables, their inherent lengths to form the word and its literary meaning influence the total effect of a musical phrase rendered through words. Thus, even when *aalaap* and *bol-aalaap* have identical note patterns and movements, they sound different because of the variety introduced by the syllables of the words and because of the mood created through its literary meaning. When the rhythmic component is changed, and the same set of notes is sung at a faster tempo, the *aalaap* and *bol-aalaap* change into *taan* and *bol-taan* and become distinct musical materials because they introduce, in an obvious way, the element of rhythm in musical phrases.

e.g., Chain of notes with rhythmic element

	N D P m G R	sargam
with vowel 'aa'	aa – – – – –	taan
with word 'sumir'	su (u) mi (i) r (a)	bol-taan

Aalaap has the potential to explore all finer aspects of a *raag* in detail. Yet *bol-s, sargam* and *taan* are also used in elaborating the *raag*. This is because of their utility in introducing 'variety' and 'novelty' in the musical material of *raag*. Thus, even though the structure of a *raag* may be treated in detail through *aalaap*, the use of other musical materials such as *bol-s, sargam* and *taan* becomes indispensible as they lend themselves to different musical effects and bring out different aspects of the *raag*'s beauty and mood.

1. *Aalaap*-s project the abstract and meditative nature of the *raag*.
2. *Bol*-s bring in variety in intonation, articulation and give specific meaning and also at times introduce the rhythmic element through the articulation of words.
3. *Taan*-s offer faster rhythmic patterns building up to a climax.
4. *Sargam* is the only musical material which can lend itself to almost any expression, movement and tempo found in *aalaap*, *bol*-s or *taan*. In addition, it expresses musical meaning and also brings in excitement.

Given this background, let me once again address myself to the question raised earlier about *sargam*.

1. Does *sargam* have any inherent qualities that makes it an aesthetically valuable expression to use in the actual performance?
2. How is *sargam* different from other musical materials such as *aalaap*, *bol*-s and *taan*?
3. What aspect of a *raag* can *sargam* portray that these other materials cannot?
4. If *sargam* is actually used in performance, how can it be sung so that it truly becomes an expression of aural beauty?

First let us examine the structure of *sargam* in comparison with *aalaap* and *taan*. The syllables *Saa, Re, Ga, Ma, Pa, Dha, Ni* have the four vowel sounds *aa, e, a, i* incorporated in them.

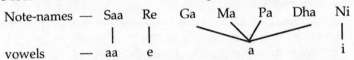

Note-names —	Saa	Re	Ga	Ma	Pa	Dha	Ni
vowels —	aa	e			a		i

After a *sargam* syllable is sung, one of these vowel sounds or formations persists, i.e., once the *sargam* syllable is uttered, what remains is the vowel in that particular syllable. It therefore takes the semblance of *aalaap*, since *aalaap* is also sung through vowels. In a sense, then, *sargam* syllables include in their structure the effect inherent in *aalaap*-s or sound carried through vowels.

By definition, *taan* is distinguished from *aalaap* by its faster pace. *Sargam* can also be used in the fast pace of *taan*-s. Thus, *sargam* includes in itself not just the vowel structure but also different tempi.

Now let us examine *sargam* in comparison with *bol*-s. *Bol-aalaap* and *bol-taan* are basically *aalaap* and *taan* combined with words. Words consist of several syllables having different lengths. The potential of these syllables in creating simple or complex rhythmic patterns as well as in imparting emotional colour to a musical phrase through the literary meaning of words must have led to the use of *bol*-s. In the process of exploring different rhythmic patterns through words, the syllables in words have to be stretched, shortened, or broken while merging them with the rhythmic melodic pattern. This naturally affects their literary integrity both in terms of sound structure and meaning. In utilising words, a singer is forced to make a compromise. He may either sing the rhythmic pattern that he wants by ignoring the literary integrity of words or he may adjust his conceived rhythmic pattern so as to keep the words intact. In other words, if the integrity of words is to be preserved in *bol*-phrases the rhythmic pattern would have to be restricted. Most of the time, when *bol*-s are used just for rhythmic play, they lose their emotional flavour and stand out as dry, meaningless structures. This may be why *bol*-s are today losing their popularity.

As against words, *sargam* has many advantages. Firstly, *sargam* consists of single syllables and secondly, it has no literary meaning. Hence, the question of distortion of word structure or neglect of literary meaning does not arise. This makes *sargam* eminently suitable for exploring complex rhythmic and melodic patterns and for conveying any emotional or aesthetic feeling desired. One may ask, how is it possible to induce emotions through the meaningless syllables of *sargam*? I will answer this question when I discuss the actual technique of singing *sargam*.

In terms of exploring the rhythmic aspect of a *raag* purely from a musical point of view, *sargam* has far more potential than either *aalaap*, *bol*-phrases and *taan*. This is because, unlike other musical materials, *sargam* is not restricted to any particular expression, movement or tempo, nor it is obstructed by the problems inherent in words. Patterns that would be difficult or impossible to sing through the other musical materials become very easy and natural in *sargam*.

For example, a phrase combining notes from three octaves involving sudden jumps like

$$\underline{NRG\ddot{G}R} \quad \underline{RSNDN} \quad \underline{NDG\ddot{R}} \quad \underline{RG\ddot{G}R} \quad \underline{\dot{S}NDPmGRS}$$

is easiest to execute gracefully through *sargam*.

We have seen how by its inherent structure, *sargam* has qualities that makes it the most suitable musical material for almost any type of expression, movement and tempo. There is yet one more significant aspect of *sargam* which makes it unique. *Sargam* as syllables not only carries vocal sound but also carries specific musical meaning. In *bol*-phrases, the musical phrase is influenced by the meaning of words. In *sargam*, the musical phrase remains purely musical because the meaning of *sargam* is related only to music. Hence, the total effect of *sargam* is significant in terms of creating an awareness of the musical activity. However, this lays responsibility on the performer to be constantly attentive in singing the right pitch while uttering *sargam* syllables. As a purely musical activity, *sargam* challenges the intelligence and offers new scope for creativity.

It must be borne in mind that the rendering of *sargam* is not a dry exercise to expose the bare skeleton of a *raag* or the mere alphabet of a musical phrase. *Sargam* in performance ought to be an expression of aural beauty, full of life, emotional colour and aesthetics. Let me now describe my conception of how *sargam* can be sung beautifully, attractively and intelligently.

Indian music does not consist of note points lying distantly apart, but of graceful lines joining these points. These lines or glides are called *meend*. *Meend* is an indispensable feature of Indian music. Expressions like *murki/harkat, khatkaa, kan, aandolan,* and *gamak* are all embellishments to make *meend* more beautiful and enchanting. However, their use is restricted to the realm of decoration, the basic ingredient for connecting the notes in a phrase being only *meend*.

What happens while singing *sargam*? If *sargam* syllables are sung as separate note-points in a phrase, they would sound like staccato notes. Does Indian music have place for such broken sounds? No, it does not. To overcome this problem, the vowels of the syllables in *sargam* are used for making glides and connecting one note-syllable with another. For example, while singing the notes *Ga* and *Ni*, the vowel '*a*' in *Ga* or vowel '*i*' in *Ni* is used to execute a connecting glide.

(i)   G   *m*   D   N
     Ga(a)————(a)Ni

vowel *'a'* in syllable *Ga* is stretched upto the pitch *Ni* and then syllable *Ni* is pronounced.

(ii)   G   m   D   N
       Ga Ni(i) ──────────i

after singing syllable *Ga* at its pitch value, syllable *Ni* is immediately sung at *Ga's* pitch value and then vowel *'i'* in *Ni* is stretched upto its pitch value.

Now this may give rise to the following objection. Is it not incorrect to extend the syllable *Ga* upto the pitch of *Ni*, when the syllable *Ga* represents only the pitch value of *Ga*?

This is where the question of skill and technique comes in. In general, the notes that are passed through by the vowels of the *sargam* syllables should be transitory and sweeping in relation to the note denoted by its syllable.

1. The glide (*meend*) makes long sweeps over the notes *R, G, m* while singing the main notes *N̤, R, G, m.*

Long sweeps —

Main notes —

2. In the *murki/harkat, S R S S* the notes of *murki* are rendered very quickly through the vowel *'aa'* of *Saa*.

       S   R S S
       Saa(aa) – – –

3. In the phrase *N D P,* the *kan* note *D* in between *N* and *P* is touched very lightly with *'i'* in *Ni*.

       N   D   P
       Ni—(i)—Pa

In all these examples, it is clear that the *sargam* syllable does not dwell upon the note. It does not signify and its vowel just passes through it or touches it during its movements to another note. While singing *sargam* with *murki*, only one *sargam* syllable is used to swiftly render a cluster of notes in a fine and delicate way for embellishment. If all the *sargam* syllables that constitute *murki* were rendered as *Saa, Re, Saa, Saa,* then *murki* would lose all its beauty.

Hence, for reasons of aesthetics and creativity, in actual performance, the rule that a *sargam* syllable should not touch a note which it does not denote is relaxed. The potential of *sargam* in rendering different kinds of clusters of notes around a central note is limitless and *sargam* makes this exploration more colourful and revealing. This process of linking the notes of a *sargam* phrase with the vowels of their syllables is not done out of ignorance but as a conscious and creative act. All types of note patterns, sequences and embellishments become transparent while rendering through *sargam*. In terms of creative potential, the use of the vowels of *sargam* syllables to sing transitory notes gives rise to numerous possibilities.

For example, while going from *Ni* to *Re*:

1. One may sing all the notes between *Ni* and *Re* with vowel '*i*' of *Ni* and land on *Re*.

$$
\begin{array}{cccccc}
N & D & P & m & G & R \\
Ni{\---}i{\---}i{\---}i{\---}i{\---}i/Re
\end{array}
$$

2. One can sing *Ni*, *Dha* and come to *Re* with the vowel '*a*' of *Dha* taking all the notes in between

$$
\begin{array}{cccccc}
N & D & P & m & G & R \\
Ni & Dha{\---}a{\---}a{\---}a{\---} a/Re
\end{array}
$$

3. One can sing the vowel '*i*' of *Ni* upto *Ma* and then sing the syllable *Re* on the pitch *Ga* and come to the pitch of *Re* with the vowel '*e*' of *Re*.

$$
\begin{array}{cccccc}
N & D & P & m & G & R \\
Ni{\---}i{\---}i{\---}i{\---}Re{\---}e
\end{array}
$$

Thus, it can be seen that the possibilities are endless.

What are the other aspects of singing *sargam* as an aesthetic tool in performance? Just as care has to be taken in preserving the literary integrity and musical quality of words through correct pronunciation, so also *sargam* syllables need to be pronounced properly to evoke a variety of aesthetic emotions.

The scope of *sargam* in the context of rhythm is far greater than in *bol*-phrases and *taan*. This is because it can include the tempi distinct to these two materials as well as use others. *Sargam* is free to explore any note pattern in any rhythm it wants because of its syllabic nature. Given this freedom, the variety and novelty integral to *sargam* is unique. It can also carry expressions, or *bhaav* which no other material can. These expressions are purely musical, in that, they are not coloured by any literary associations.

The rendering of *sargam* today has been influenced by instrumental as well as Karnatak music. *Sargam* can carry expressions which are typical to string instruments, like the *sitaar*, in terms of its subtle movement of notes, spectacular note patterns, amazing flights through all three octaves and complicated yet playful gait. For instance, *sargam* can simulate *taan*-s which sound very much like *jhaalaa*. *Sargam* has also been influenced by Karnatak music. Its typical way of swinging notes and using staccato like stresses in line with rhythm have entered Hindustani music through *sargam*.

We have seen that *sargam* has a wide range in terms of combinations, tempi, expressions and effects. During practice it may be sung in a simple way as mere alphabets, but in performance it must be given expression through the right use of glides and ornamentations. *Sargam* challenges the intelligence of both performer and listener. When the search for beauty and novelty through *sargam* yields fruit, it gives tremendous joy to both. There are certain delicate turns and complex movements that even connoisseurs at times fail to perceive. *Sargam* at this point becomes a means of interpretation and communicates more directly the artist's intention. It makes his intricate movements, patterns and overall design, easier to grasp and hence easier to appreciate.

Because of its manifold nature, *sargam* singing today has become very popular and except in folk music, it has crept into practically every type of music from classical, light-classical to light, film, theatre and even pop and disco music.

In my view, Indian classical vocal music fulfils itself through *sargam*, in that, *sargam* is able to do what other musical materials cannot. Music in its purest form simply consists of notes and rhythm. Through *sargam*, vocal music is able to relieve itself from the literary aspect of words and concentrate solely upon directly communicating the musical meaning of music.

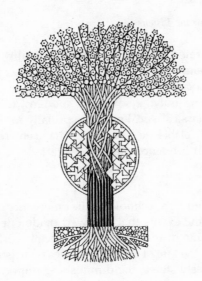

7

KHYAAL AND MODERNITY

Our technological age is continuously bringing us closer and closer. Total isolation, even if we were to desire it, is no longer possible. This closeness, in a way, is constantly providing new surroundings to the creative minds. They seem to draw or discard, consciously or otherwise, from the surrounding context, and the results are—new materials, new techniques, new patterns, new movements, and new expressions. When we look at the performing arts against this background, we are amazed by the possibilities that are present before us.

As a professional classical singer, I am directly and continuously involved with the creative aspect of music. I have often mused over certain things that have been termed as 'modern' in North Indian classical vocal music, especially in 'khyaal'.

What is modernity? How and why does it originate? Does it or does it not merge with the parent stream of tradition? These and similar questions keep us thinking all the time. Scholars in various fields have, at one time or another, answered these questions, or rather in their attempts to provide answers, thrown useful light on them; for in the sphere of art, no questions have final answers or need to be answered with finality. They are open ended. It is enough to examine them, ponder over them, in which process many a cobweb is brushed away.

While pointing out the so called 'modern' things in today's North Indian classical vocal music, especially in *'khyaal'* singing, I will also briefly elaborate on why they have entered into classical music and what influence they have exerted.

BACKGROUND

The advent of modern technology, the emergence of India's independence and the events that followed made one realise afresh, about how events in the political and social world affect, in an important way, the fate of art and the lives of artists. The merging of the old princely states, the diminishing importance of dance, drama and music in the regular cycles of worship in temples, the growing influence of Western ways in life styles, the tendency of the wealthy and the elite to use their dealings with art and the artist as status symbols, the general inadequacy of Government and public policies towards the arts and ineffective implementation of these policies have all tended to drive the arts to the common man's support for survival. On the other hand, the new senses of national identity and national pride have engendered more warmth towards the classical traditions in the arts. The seeds of modernity in the Indian arts are to be found here.

TRADITION

It must be remembered that what was sung as 'traditional' by the previous generation had itself evolved through the centuries. Music of these previous generations reveals the impact of their times and the adjustments they had to make to keep pace with the artistic needs of their generation. If it is agreed that art must show an awareness of changing times and its needs; it follows that changes in art forms must be deemed not only inevitable, but also vitally necessary. Classical music must, therefore, be considered in the context of its times.

CONTRIBUTION OF LISTENERS

In the evolution, preservation, propagation and progress of music through the centuries, its listeners have contributed to its course no less than the musicians themselves. A special feature of Indian music concerts is an active participation of the listeners in the creation of music during the performance through their body language and appreciative verbal responses. There exists and has always existed, a sort of continuous dialogue between a sensitive performer and discerning listeners; and the music has moulded and remoulded itself as a result of their mutual responses. From the earliest Vedic chant to the present *khyaal* we see one long, continuous march, where the old and the new are linked together. When music began to be used mainly for entertainment, the artist's primary objective became that of furnishing his patrons with ever fresh novelties. In the race to do this, while on the one hand many practices disruptive of tradition became current, on the other, many thoughtful and responsible artists enriched tradition with new features of vigour and beauty.

KHYAAL

Today's North Indian classical vocal music is obviously represented by *khyaal*. The voice of *dhrupad-dhamaar* is no doubt heard occasionally, but it is regarded more as an 'ancestor 'of the *khyaal* than as its contemporary. *Khyaal* has been in vogue for over two hundred years, but it too could not escape the transformations which were inevitable with the changing listeners. At one time it revealed a close kinship to *dhrupad-dhamaar*, but over the years it has undergone such radical transformation that it reminds one of the transformation of a caterpillar into a butterfly. Freedom is its watch-word, infinity its domain. It tends to be all comprehensive, receptive of almost everything. The fight that *khyaal* has put up against various encroachments made by film music, theatre music, folk music, instrumental music, Karnatak music, Western music and science and technology is very interesting and worth taking notice of.

Ideas about tradition, beauty etc., are inculcated in one's mind because of their acceptance through generations; they are more often blindly borrowed; critical thinking is hardly involved. With the increased number of branches of science, the scope of experience has also widened. Science directed man to take an objective view of life. There now prevails a spirit of enquiry which does not easily accept the authority of tradition without subjecting it to the test of reason, to one's independent thought and experience. When the frame of established rules and regulations obstructed freedom of expression, it is inevitably battered, loosened and finally broken down.

RAAG AND TAAL

The concepts of *raag* and *taal* which are the unique features of Indian music have been moulding and maturing themselves in accordance with the needs of time. *Vaadi, samvaadi, thaat,* etc., which form the grammar of a *raag* are becoming less and less important. The artist is now mainly concerned with the notes of the scale of *raag*, their characteristic ascending-descending movements, core phrases and mainly his own interpretation of the *raag*—its personality as a whole. This attitude has influenced the smaller details in the development and presentation of a *raag*. Every note is being given an exhaustive treatment in the context of the *raag* of which it forms a part. Thus, the subtle embroidery or filigree work on the notes is on the increase. This has resulted in a comparatively slow tempo of the *taal* for *vilambit* (slow) *khyaal*. The tendency to ignore *taal* especially in *aalaap*-s (slow phrases) thus has its roots in avoiding obstruction by the tempo and segments of the *taal* frame. As slow speed has made filigree work on the notes in *aalaap*-s possible, the extreme fast speed of *taal* has added an element of surprise and thrill in the performance. Modern sound projection systems with their special types of microphones have made it possible to convey even the subtlest nuances of singing, instrument playing to the audience, in a very clear and crisp manner. Artists therefore delight in creating such filigree patterns of delicacy and win appreciation from the audience.

BANDISH OR PRE-COMPOSED SONG OR TUNE REDUCED TO ONE TIME CYCLE

Indian music has lived through the oral tradition. In this tradition the *bandish* or the pre-composed song assumed great importance since it contained in seed-form a rendering of a particular *raag* and form. It thus provided, in a way, guidelines to the artist in realising the *raag* and projecting the form. However, it also indirectly put restrictions on the artist to be within the tonal structure of the *bandish* or word composition. Today's artist wishes to experience the *raag*, free from this restriction. Secondly, *khyaal* being an abstract form, the artist wants to build its structure only with 'pure' musical constituents—*swara* and *laya* and avoid words which colour the phrase with specific meaning. As a result of this feeling, the length of the text, especially in *vilambit* or slow *khyaal* is getting smaller. The second half of the composition—*antaraa* is disappearing fast and the first part—*sthaayi*—too generally consists of one cycle of *taal*. However, although the composition of words is getting smaller, the rendering of *raag* is becoming more emotional and romantic and words of the composition are being exploited for this purpose.

SARGAM

Another noticeable difference in the *raag* presentation today is the growing use of *sargam* in place of *bol*-phrases. One reason for this could be that the composition of words has become short; another could be that in *bol*-phrases the words had to be broken into parts and consequently their emotional content had to be sacrificed. In *sargam* (solfaggios), *Saa, Re, Ga, Ma* are the meaning-ful alphabets in the language of music. They convey musical meaning and aesthetic emotions of the musical phrases. Moreover, the note patterns which appear difficult or impossible in *aalaap* and *taan* can be rendered with ease through *sargam* because of their mono-syllabic nature. It is interesting to note that not only in *khyaal* but also in word oriented forms like *thumri, daadraa, ghazal, bhajan,* film, theatre, pop, disco, and fusion music *sargam* is used freely and with gay abandon.

SCIENCE AND TECHNOLOGY

The twentieth century ushered in an era of science and technology and it affected life in all its totality. It was a comparatively speedy change and an all-prevailing one. Naturally, its echoes were heard in the field of art too.

In music, various media such as radio, TV, films, theatre, audio, video, cassettes, and CDs brought different types of music, ranging from Western to folk, close to the people at large. Consequently in a very short span of time, these media created a demand for different kinds of music as the number of listener-viewers in-creased rapidly. Naturally, the members of this audience were on different levels of music awareness. Their tastes were different, their expectations from music were different.

Science also brought a major difference in the artist-audience relationship. While TV transformed music into a 'visual art', the microphone increased the physical distance between the two and affected the level of artistic communication which was so vital in the creation of music during the actual performance. A new society was born where the artist looked at his art as a saleable commodity and the audience perceived art as a piece of entertainment. This marks a significant attitudinal change from earlier times when art was sacrosanct and the artist, a figure of near divinity.

MICROPHONE

Not only do the ideas of beauty change but also the methods of its appreciation change according to the changing times. Before the microphone arrived on the scene, a voice which could be heard in the most distant corner of a hall was considered good. Naturally, the artistic work on the notes had to be such that it could be heard by all. The loudness of the voice being an essential feature, the notes tended to be straight, bold and the speed of phrases slow. The microphone brought about revolution in music. Audibility no longer remained a problem; even a breath could be heard. The tonal quality of sound assumed great importance. The artist began to think in terms of making conscious use of volume, timbre, range and speed to increase the communicative ability of his voice. The embroidery work on the notes of the *aalaap* began to be more delicate and subtle; the *taan*-s moved with jet speed, the combination of notes in the phrases became more complicated.

FILM MUSIC

Film is the medium today which offers a variety of entertainment at minimum expense. From village to metropolitan cities every nook and corner of the country is under its spell. Music is a major and important part of the Indian films. Its production is on a very large scale and it also gets tremendous publicity. Whether one wishes or not, one is forced to listen to it through the TV, portable transistors on the roads or at public places.

It reaches people of different strata of society with great ease. It thus pervades the emotional life of the society as a whole. The classical musicians and audience too have not been able to remain impervious to the effects of film music.

Either it is a coincidence or a result of a conscious search for good voices; the film industry is fortunate in getting highly sensitive, expressive, emotional and mellifluous voices for playback singing. The voices of these playback singers came to be compared consciously or unconsciously with the voices of classical musicians. This resulted in the classical singers paying more attention to their voices. Earlier the quality of voice did not matter much; it was mainly the knowledge, technique and skill which won recognition. A good voice now became an essential tool of a classical singer and the fear of instant rejection made him conscious of his voice quality. He endeavoured to make his voice better and more effective. The idea of varying the texture of voice by manipulating timbre and volume, making it soft, whispery, bold, pointed, broad, open, guttural, husky, etc., is now finding favour with classical musicians. There is another indication of the effect of film music on classical singing. The practice of singing in a very high pitch, of trying to reach notes in higher octaves has become a musical gimmick which earns sure applause.

Since film music has the background of a story and action, words and emotional expression become very important. This stressed the importance of words on the minds of classical singers too and their pronunciation of words became clearer, pointed, graceful and emotional. While concentrating on grammar, they now sang with an awareness for beauty and feelings. Another direct result of the effect of film music was that 'love' which plays a major role in film music began to abound in classical songs too. The male-female duets in film music have made an appearance in the concerts of classical music where two artists sing together from the same platform. There is an element of competition in what is commonly known as *'jugalbandi'*, but today, *jugalbandi* has become *'yugal sangeet'*, where the artists sing or play in a way which is complementary to each other. This has also affected the content, expression and presentation in classical music.

The variety in *thekaa* of a *taal* is yet another contribution of film music. These new *thekaa*-s (commonly known as 'patterns' in the world of film rhythmists) in turn have influenced not only the tonal contour of the word composition or text but also the progression in the development of the form. Thus film music has contributed in many ways. On one hand, it has made classical musicians aware of the tonal quality of voice, pronunciation of words, expression of feeling, clarity and neatness in presentation, and on the other hand, trained the ears of the common man in terms of tunefulness, beauty of voice and finish and polish in overall presentation.

THEATRE MUSIC

Classical music in Maharashtra exhibits a novel touch of theatre music. The theatre music originated in folk music and classical music, but it gradually developed its own style and identity. The theatre artist-singer had an advantage. Like the film, the play had a story and a stage setting to suit the mood of the song. The song was intrinsically woven into the action of the play. It also had literary merit. To add to this, acting and singing on the stage was a live performance.

The theatre songs (*naatya sangeet*)were sung by artists like Bal Gandharva who had a halo of glamour around them. As a result of all this, theatre music had a profound impact on the minds of the people at large. It began to attract massive audience patronage. Classical singers were naturally attracted towards the style of theatre music which made an altogether different and novel attempt to move the hearts of the spectators and audience. The characteristic musical mannerisms of the theatre singers, their style of rendering *taan*, tendency to repeat a line of the song with different variations and such other features of stage music were gradually introduced into classical music that came from Maharashtra.

FOLK MUSIC

Folk music is a natural expression of the human mind and has perpetually inspired other types of music. After independence, folk music once again gained its place of honour in the cultural life of the people and continued to enrich contemporary classical music. Musicians reflected upon certain '*dhun*-s' or melodies in folk music in the context of the *raag*-s, forms and themes. The abandon, spontaneity and free expression of folk music, its beauty and simplicity, its rustic quality and enticing rhythm, its excitement and intoxication have mesmerized even the classical musicians. This induction of the folk type into classical music has given it a renewed vigour and mass appeal. Today ethnic music forms a special class of music in the market.

INSTRUMENTAL MUSIC

In India, vocal music enjoys a higher place than instrumental music. May be for this reason instrumental music did not, for a long time, make any noticeable progress as an independent medium and more or less remained under the shadow of vocal music. However, in recent years instrumental music has developed a style of its own which is strikingly different from that of vocal music. The instrumentalists realized the inherent qualities of their instruments and began to make skilful use of these qualities in their performance.The novelty in the expression of instrumental music and the popularity earned by the artist have forced the vocalist to think about instrumental music differently. The instrumentalist trying to imitate the voice on his instrument is not new. Today the vocalist also tries to produce typical expressions of the instrument. Though both vocal and instrumental musicians realise their respective limitations, they try to draw close to one another retaining their identity. The influence of instruments like *sitaar* and *sarod* in the rendering of vocal music can be noticed through such things as the swings of notes, very fast tempo *'jhaalaa'* type *taan*-s and the growing popularity of *sargam*, which enables the artist to produce combinations and expressions formerly typical of instrumental music.

KARNATAK MUSIC

Indian music has two main systems of music. The music in North India is Hindustani music while the music in South India is Karnatak music. Although the concepts of *raag* and *taal* are common to both, there is a difference in approach, technique, expression and presentation. Today these two systems are seen complementing and enriching each other. The exchange of *raag*-s has started long ago. Even some of the compositions have been borrowed without any change. But now, the expressions and stylistic details in these two systems have begun to exercise an influence over one another. For instance, in Hindustani music, the touch of Karnatak style is evident in the rendering of *'gamak*-s'.

Now, a new and rare possibility for an exchange and enrichment of musical expression has been created by the artists of
Hindustani and Karnatak music coming together for *'jugalbandi'*.
Expansion and development in the media exposed listeners of
each style to the other. Earlier, language was a major obstacle in
confronting music of the other style. Instrumental music on radio,
TV, cassettes, CDs, etc., brought it to the notice of the listeners
that the Northern and Southern styles have several musical
elements in common. This also helped in removing the alienation
between North and South and brought them closer.

FORMS

In the modes of exposition of *raag*-s, a number of forms came into
existence to suit the needs of the changing times. Some of these
forms were lost during the passage of time. Some managed to go
ahead by adapting themselves to the needs. *Dhrupad-dhamaar,
khyaal, taraanaa, tappaa, thumri, daadraa, geet, ghazal,* and *bhajan* are
some of the contemporary classical, light-classical and light forms
in Hindustani music. All these forms have their own stylistic
features. Today, their dividing lines are getting thinner. Even the
schools of *khyaal* and *thumri* are slowly disappearing. Every artist
picks up what appeals to him from all the styles and makes use
of it according to his ability. Especially, those artists who present
only one type of music in their concert are seen consciously incorporating the features of other forms to make their music more
entertaining. The classical *khyaal* now displays a close affinity to
light classical *thumri*. The *murki*-s and the *khatkaa*-s in *thumri* are
now used with abandon in *khyaal*. The *sargam* and the *taan* can
now be heard in *thumri*. The light form *ghazal* has now come
closer to *khyaal* and *thumri* by incorporating spacious *aalaap*-s,
taan-s and *sargam*-s. This exchange of styles amongst different
forms is a continuous process.

WESTERN MUSIC

Since British rule, Western music has exercised an influence on
Indian artists and audiences who have imbibed it consciously or
unconsciously. Western music has a large sway over Indian film
music. Even light music seems to have gone under its hold.
However, classical music has remained unaffected, mainly because

the concept of harmony in Western music is alien to the concept of melody in Indian classical music. To introduce harmony into Indian classical music, one has to face the problem of having to reduce the *raag* to its scale. The scale assumes the personality of a *raag* by the way in which its notes are combined and expressed through *meend* and *gamak*-s. The concept of *raag* stands on pure, bare melody.

As a novelty, no doubt an illusion of harmony is created even in Hindustani classical music by sounding the chords on the accompanying instruments while main artist is steady on a particular note.

Similarly in *sargam* rendering, when the note-names are patterned on the line of chords and pronounced in a particular way, it is sought to create an illusion akin to harmony. However, this is being done on a very very limited scale.

An important aspect of the global encounter is that the *raag* is losing its rigidity. This change can be seen in the different approaches possible in terms of its materials, techniques, patterns, and expressions. These changes are very subtle but a sensitive ear and analytical mind can perceive them occurring.

CONCLUDING

When one views the encroachments made on classical or *raag* music or its representative form *khyaal*; by film, folk, Karnatak, instrumental and Western music and science and technology, one finds these encroachments to be at a peripheral, superficial level. They have not affected the 'soul' of *raag* or *khyaal*. These outside encroachments have not only enhanced the beauty of a *raag* or *khyaal* but have also prolonged its life.

Hindustani classical music today is subjected to two kinds of contradictory accusations. On one hand, the critics clamour, in the name of theory and tradition, that "the standard of classical music has deteriorated and that it has not retained its original purity". On the other hand, it is argued that "classical music has become static, that it is not taking new strides in tune with the changing times". To say that "old is gold" or to argue that whatever is old should be totally rejected are two extreme view-points. Creative modernity lies in exploring new paths without losing the base or essence of tradition. That classical music must change and adapt itself to new ideas for survival, is inevitable. In fact, classical music assimilated new trends into its mainstream whenever the artists have found it necessary. However, it must be remembered that only those trends have been assimilated which have been in tune with the basic thought and structure of classical music. *Khyaal* which represents *raag* music wishes to survive and retain its identity even as it changes to make itself more exciting and emotionally satisfying. Nourished by its old roots, *khyaal* is scaling to new heights and this is modernity—the recognition of the need to change with the times.

Khansaheb Abdul Karim Khan

8

KIRANA *GHARAANAA*

To sing is a natural human impulse. When music springs spontaneously from the folk mind and passes through a more deliberate aesthetic shaping process, art music is evolved.

The art music of India is but one of the many genres evolved by the civilizations of the world. Each has a different material, approach, structure, and expression. Indian music, followed the path of melody (using a succession of notes one after another and not many notes at the same instance). In the search for a higher form of melody and rhythm, after centuries of creative thinking and experimentation, it blossomed into *raag* (tone-structure) and *taal* (time-structure). These are the two concepts, two distinctive characteristics of Indian music.

In the expression of a *raag*, there appeared a number of forms to meet the demands of changing time.

The *khyaal* is today's most popular vocal form representing *raag* music. Since there was no written music, but only a basic frame of *raag* and form crystallized in a *bandish* (a pre-composed tune), the artist had full freedom to choose his material and manner of expression. This freedom gave rise to various ideologies which came to be known as *gharaanaa*-s in *khyaal*.

The word *'gharaanaa'* used in *khyaal* singing suggests a 'family' of artists with a particular attitude, following a particular style. This style is broadly based on ideology, voice-production and technique, and is handed down from master to pupil through oral instructions. However, while remaining within the tradition of his *gharaanaa*, the artist often borrows consciously or unconsciously, ideas from other *gharaanaa*-s that can be assimilated easily, and thus enriches his own style and his *gharaanaa*.

In Indian music, the basic constituents of music—*swara* and *laya* undergo a specific treatment and appear in two kinds of phrases—*'aalaap'* and *'taan'*. In vocal music one more component—'word' with or without meaning becomes inevitable. Thus, the basic material—*swara*, *laya* and words after processing transforms itself into four kinds of phrases.

1. *Aalaap*—slow lingering phrases usually rhythm free.
2. *Bol-s*—phrases with words from the song-text with or without rhythm.
3. *Sargam*—phrases with abbreviated note-names with or without rhythm (solfaggios).
4. *Taan*—fast phrases usually rhythm bound (a speedy succession of notes).

In the present discussion, I will restrict myself to describe only the Kirana *gharaanaa* as my music has roots there.

The Kirana *gharaanaa* which rose above the horizon of tradition with Ustad Abdul Karim Khansaheb's singing, continues to attract lay and initiated listeners alike. Its growing popularity with the listeners and the increasing number of its followers, have given it an enviable place among *gharaanaa*-s of our times.

The *gharaanaa* is named 'Kirana' after a place of the same name in North India, near Delhi. Abdul Karim Khan was born in Kirana. Trends that shaped the musical character of this *gharaanaa* must have started earlier; but it was in Khansaheb's hands that it became mature and popular.

Khansaheb's music cast a hypnotic spell on those who thronged to hear him. It was a yearning of the soul—it was the compelling music that 'Shastras' talked about— *'shishurvethi, pashurvethi'*, ('the child knows it; the animal knows it'). Khansaheb used to say he sang *'gobarhaari baani'* a style which flourished in the golden age of *dhrupad*.

Being a good *been* player, his involvement with the strings was very deep. It made his voice sensitive to *swara*-s and *shruti*-s (microtones). The voice, the emotional expression, the slow expansive *aalaap*, the *sargam*—all became a part of Kirana *gaayaki*. Khansaheb sang with all his soul; the technique involved was beneath the surface.

Ustad Abdul Waheed Khan, a nephew of Khansaheb, met this aesthetic wave in a manner which was more technical, analytical, and methodical. Kirana thereafter followed the path which these two great artists had laid down receiving the impacts of the times.

Kirana's basic structure has not changed over the years. Its main asset is its sweetness of tone, its general soothing effect on the mind. Having realised the importance of the voice, it has developed its own technique of voice-production, which draws even lay listeners towards classical music. "Music is an art first, and then a science. The possibility of instant rejection by the listener is always there if voice - the medium - is poor", says a Kirana singer. Noticeable emotional content is another element in its mass appeal.

The slow spacious *aalaap*-s include *meend, kan, khatkaa*, and *gamak*. This is mainly an influence from the instruments *been* and *saarangi*, played by the forefathers of Kirana. Being a *swara* oriented style, it develops each note of the *raag* step by step in the context of that particular *raag*. This kind of elaboration or improvisation highlighting the presence of the note is characteristic to the Kirana style.

The caressing of the notes does not allow any aggressive attitude towards *taal*. The strikingly slow *laya* (tempo), often favoured, gives a peculiar sense of repose, which creates a peaceful atmosphere in which the listeners see the *raag* grow like a tree branch by branch, leaf by leaf, flower by flower, fruit by fruit. The focus on the finer shades of notes and their combinations inevitably demands a slower tempo of the *taal*. This has led to the criticism that "Kirana neglects *taal* both as structure and as tempo." To this the Kirana reply is that "the phrases can have their own structure, movements and pace, different from *taal* structure and its pace." Thus to avoid continuous obstruction, the *taal* is allowed to remain at a slow pace. It therefore runs under the phrases, giving them support, meeting them at times and at the *'sam'* (the first beat of *taal* cycle which gets focused in the musical composition). The use of *taal* in a *vilambit khyaal* is therefore far more subdued than in other *gharaanaa*-s.

Secondly, although very sensitive to the emotional content in general, Kirana is not very careful about the words of the *bandish*, their pronunciation, their meaning. Words come as part of the musical material losing their identity. Limited use of words and *taal* is reflected in the absence of *bol*-phrases with rhythm. Kirana has been using mostly traditional *bandish*-s. But today the situation has changed. Quite a few artists have started composing their own *bandish*-s which have become very popular.

The use of '*sargam*' with its affinity to the Karnatak style was a novelty during Khansaheb's time. Other *gharaanaa*-s practically ignored this component. Even Kirana's own followers did not show much love for *sargam* till recently. Today *sargam* has become almost a weakness with many singers even outside Kirana *gharaanaa*.

As to the *taan*, one sees an increasing urge towards clarity, variety, complexity, rhythmic vigour, and speed from Khansaheb to later generations. Kirana's attempt to bring Hindustani and Karnatak music closer is commendable. In addition to adapting Karnatak melodies to Hindustani music, it also adapted certain '*gamak*-s' and gave a new flavour to its music. It is interesting to note that a sizable number of Kirana artists came from Hubli and Dharwar in Karnataka state. A style which had its roots in North India flowered in the South.

Such are some of the features of the Kirana *gharaanaa* today. Its future course will depend mainly on the audience response and the influence of technology. The boundary lines between existing *gharaanaa*-s are getting less and less rigid and there is much overlapping. The artist's fight for freedom, the attitude of listeners, the inevitable commercial element, all these will shape the content, manner and expression of *khyaal* in general and of each *gharaanaa* in particular.

Apart from its mentors Ustad Abdul Karim Khan and Abdul Waheed Khan, the Kirana *gharaanaa* has a galaxy of outstanding musicians. It is a matter of pride that there are numerous youngsters who have embraced this style and are carrying the torch of Kirana tradition into the future.

9

Thumri—A Light-Classical Vocal Genre towards Abstraction

Radha's anklets
on her feet,
Krishna's flute
in her hands,
Meera's deep love
in her breath,
the soul's plaintive cry
on her lips,
the bliss of union
in her eyes,
thumri moves
onward on her path
to the temple
of the Formless.

During its long history, Indian music has been expressing itself through various forms. The selection, treatment, expression and presentation of the music material gave each form its identity.

Many ancient musical forms have possibly undergone changes through assimilation of influences from different sources and reappeared in a new garb and new identity. Enterprising musicians have been continuously engaged in moulding contemporary forms to meet the demands of changing times. The vocal form - *thumri* is one such form which has strong links with folk music and has flowered as an art form. Folk music has always been a great source of inspiration for art music and has enriched art music in terms of musical material, style, expression and themes.

Material of Music

The material of music consists of tone and time. There is one more component in vocal music - words, which become part of the musical material. Knowing that human beings can produce sound mainly through vowels and consonants (clapping, whis-tling, humming, etc., are also ways of producing sound; but they have limitations), Indian musicians have intelligently explored a variety of expressions through words—words with meaning and syllables without meaning.

Words are meaningful arrangement of sound signals which form the main core of vocal utterances. The tonal variety of consonants and feature of length associated with the vowels create a kind of musicality in the spoken form of the word itself. Man must have realised this and tried to enhance it through its adap-tation to the musical form. Indeed, words have helped in bringing variety and novelty into the musical material of vocal music. In vocal music, musical material comprises four types of phrases— *aalaap, taan, sargam,* and *bol*-s. In the last category, *bol*-s, i.e., phrases with words, there are five sub-varieties—*bol-aalaap, bol-upaj, bol-taan, bol-banaav,* and *bol-baant.* As these phrases are with syllables or words from the pre-composed song, they help in bringing variety in articulation, introducing a rhythmic element and also in lending a specific emotional colour to the phrases.

In *bol-aalaap, bol-upaj,* and *bol-taan,* the primary function of words/syllables is to bring variety in articulation and help in rhythmic manipulation. The literary meaning or emotional content of the words has secondary place in these phrases. In *bol-banaav,* and *bol-baant,* there is a conscious effort all the time to compose phrases in such a way to project the emotional content of the words. *Bol-banaav* has leisurely movements while *bol-baant* includes rhythmic movements. Thus each type of *bol*-phrases, *bol-aalaap*, *bol-upaj*, *bol-taan*, *bol-banaav*, and *bol-baant*, has a distinct quality and its own utility in the making of music.

VOCAL FORMS—RAAG AND WORDS

Besides bringing variety in the musical material, words have also played an important role in the creation of forms in vocal music. The classification of art forms into three categories—classical, light-classical, and light is based on the relative importance of *raag* or words or both in a particular form. Each form selects its material and moulds it in a specific way in terms of tonal texture, design, technique, expression of aesthetic or literary emotions and overall presentation. For example, *aalaap*-s in *dhrupad* differ from *aalaap*-s in *khyaal* and *thumri*. *Taan*-s in *khyaal* differ from *taan*-s in *tappaa*. *Bol-upaj* in *dhrupad* differs from *bol-upaj* in *khyaal*, and *bol-baant* and *bol-banaav* are special to *thumri* only.

FORM - THUMRI

The vocal form *thumri* has been placed in the light-classical category because of its close attention to both *raag* and words. *Raag* oriented phrases in *thumri* compose themselves to protect the meaning of the words, while words stretch artistically and beautifully to fit into the characteristic phrases and expression of the form. Words give specific meaning to the phrases while *raag* becomes the basis of improvisation or elaboration of the text and development of the form. Thus words and *raag* complement each other and still retain their identity. *Raag* itself suggests a colour— 'that which colours is a *raag*', says the traditional definition of *raag*. When this colour is matched with a particular shade of expression in the word/in the text, the aesthetic experience is even more beautiful.

The association of *thumri* with dance in the beginning led to emphasis on *bol-baant*, i.e., rhythmic treatment of the text. When *thumri* stepped on the concert platform, its emphasis shifted to the melodic treatment of the text, i.e., *bol-banaav*. In this process of transition from *bol-baant* to *bol-banaav*, the tempo of *thumri* slowed down considerably to allow rhythm-free phrases. These phrases knowingly/unknowingly tried to free themselves from the words. The flexible, dissolvable text of *thumri* indeed helped this process. Since then *thumri* has slowly been evolving as an abstract musical form relatively independent of words and their meaning.

THUMRI TEXT AND ITS TREATMENT

Thumri texts are simple and use a limited stock of words. There is no identifiable literary form or strict pattern as in the texts of *geet*, *ghazal*, and *bhajan*. Secondly, the integrity of the word structure in *thumri* is not as high as in *geet*, *ghazal*, *bhajan*-s. Words stretch themselves to fit into the characteristic phrases. Thirdly, the emotions in *thumri* texts are broad based. The texts expressing opposite sentiments—joy, sorrow, etc., use the same stereotyped melodic structure for *mukhdaa* and the same melodic phrases and ornamentations for the elaboration of the text. All this contributes to the easy musical manipulation of the text and in turn to the abstract potential of *thumri*.

For example:

Same melodic contour for different themes:

A. *Raag Kaafi*
 (i) *'Piyaa to maanata naahi'* — He is not listening to me

S	R	R	g	R	M	M	P	P
Pi	yaa	to	maa	–	na	ta	naa	hi

 (ii) *'Khelata Nandakumaar'* — Nandakumar (Lord Krishna) is playing Holi

S	R	R	g	R	M	M	P	P
Khe	la	ta	Nan	–	da	ku	maa	r

B. *Raag Khamaaj*
 (i) *'Kona gali gayo Shyaam'*— Which way has my beloved Shyam (Lord Krishna) gone

G	G	M	G	R	G	M	P	P
Ko	na	ga	li	–	ga	yo	Shyaa	m

 (ii) *'Aisi naa maaro pichakaari'* — Please don't throw colour on me

G	G	M	G	R	G	M	P	P
Ai	si	naa	maa	ro	pi	cha	kaa	ri

Same melodic phrase for words having opposite meaning:

A. *Raag Des*

R M P N Ṡ N Ṡ₁ n D P

(i) ₁aa - - - - - -₁ vo - -   'aavo' (come)

(ii) ₁jaa - - - - - -₁ vo - -   'jaavo' (go)

B. *Raag Pilu*

(i) 'Jaadu daalaa' — He has done magic

R ₁g R g₁ ₁S R S R g R₁ S Ṇ

Jaa ₁du - -₁ ₁daa - - - - -₁ laa -

(ii) 'Jiyaa laage naa' — Restless I am without him

R ₁g R g₁ ₁S R S R g R₁ S Ṇ

Ji ₁yaa - -₁ ₁laa - - - - ge₁ naa -

Same melodic contour in different forms and different *taal*-s:

'Mitawaa maanata naahi, naahi re' — *mukhadaa* line of the song-text in *raag Kaafi*

(i) *Chotaa khyaal* in *Teentaal* - also - *daadraa* in *taal Keherwaa* (16 beats)

1	2	3	4	5	6	7	8	9	10	11	12	13	14	15	16
X				2				0				3			
								–	M	₁PnD₁	₁D P₁	g	R	M	M
								–	Mi	₁ta - -₁	₁waa -₁	maa	–	na	ta
P	–	–	M	M	PDP	g	R								
naa	–	–	hi	naa	₁- - hi₁	re	–								

(ii) *Thumri* in *taal Deepchandi* - also - *dhamaar* in *taal Dhamaar* (14 beats)

1	2	3	4	5	6	7	8	9	10	11	12	13	14
X			2				0			3			
							M	₁PnD₁	₁D P₁	g	₁RgSR₁	M	M
							Mi	₁ta - -₁	₁waa -₁	maa	₁- - - -₁	na	ta
P	–	–	₁D PMP₁	₁MPDP₁	g	R							
naa	–	hi	₁naa - - -₁	₁- - hi₁	re	–							

(iii) *Daadraa* in *taal Daadraa* (6 beats)

1	2	3	4	5	6	1	2	3	4	5	6
X			0			X			0		
M	₁PnD₁	₁D P₁	₁g R₁	M	M	P	–	p	M	₁PD P₁	₁g R₁
Mi	₁ta - -₁	₁waa -₁	₁maa -₁	na	ta	naa	–	hi	naa	₁- - hi₁	₁re -₁

(iv) *Khyaal/thumri* in *Jhap taal* (10 beats)

1	2	3	4	5	6	7	8	9	10
X		2			0		3		
M	D P	n D	D	P	g	R	M	–	M
Mi	ta –	– –	waa	–	ma	–	na	–	ta
P	–	MP	MPD	P	g	R	g	S	R
naa	–	– –	– – –	hi	re	–	–	–	–

(v) *Khyaal/thumri* in *taal Rupak* (7 beats)

1	2	3	4	5	6	7	1	2	3	4	5	6	7
X			2		3		X			2		3	
M	PnD	D P	g	R	M	M	P	–	P	MD	P	g	R
Mi	ta – –	waa –	maa	–	na	ta	naa	–	hi	naa –	hi	re	–

- one comes across so many others of the same type.

By and large, the themes and the words in classical and light-classical art forms are the same. It is, therefore, possible to use the same word composition with slight changes to suit only the rhythmic pattern of different forms under the two categories—classical (*dhrupad* or *khyaal*) and light-classical (*thumri* or *daadraa*). The melodic structure of the same word composition however will differ with each form due to the *taal* structure, tempo, characteristic phrases and their expression. In light music, the word composition itself represents a complete form; elaboration of the form is incidental and not a necessity. In classical and light-classical categories the word composition is only a part of the musical material of the form and unless the characteristic musical phrases are woven around the word composition, the form remains incomplete. The fact that these characteristic musical phrases can be rendered without words or by using meaningless words and can also be played without words on an instrument shows that the words can be ignored to establish the *thumri* form. Needless to say that words will lend specific meaning to the phrases in vocal *thumri* and enrich its overall expression. From this angle vocalists will always have the upper hand over instrumentalists. They will be able to express specific emotions through words.

RAAG

Thumri generally uses the so called 'light' *raag*-s having close links with folk tunes. But for text elaboration most of the time it borrows phrases from serious *raag*-s. Of course these phrases are moulded to suit *thumri* expressions. The point to be stressed here is that, in addition to the inherent potential of the scale of the *raag*, it is also the 'treatment' of the melodic material of the *raag* in a particular way which makes it 'light' or 'heavy'. It may also be noted that the so called 'light *raag*-s' themselves are maturing as time passes and *khyaal* singers and instrumentalists today are treating quite a few of them as 'major' *raag*-s. Thus, although for projecting the literary emotions expressed in the *thumri* text, the singer takes inspiration from the words, he leans on the *raag* and its aesthetic emotions for elaboration of the form. Not only this, but he must also know well how to shift artistically from one *raag* into another using the typical expressions and ornamentations of the form without loss to the homogeneity of the total structure. At this point *raag* itself becomes the source of inspiration in *thumri*.

FORMS IN LIGHT-CLASSICAL CATEGORY

Daadraa is another important form in the light-classical category. There is a lot of confusion about what is *thumri* and what is *daadraa*, because apart from the tempo, both the forms use the same *raag*-s and the same *taal*-s, project similar themes, and even use the same melodic phrases and expressions in the elaboration. *Thumri* is comparatively slow, while *daadraa* has a lilting rhythm. The tempo influences the structure of the text composition and the movements of the phrases in the elaboration. The difference between *thumri* and *daadraa* is exactly like the difference between *badaa* and *chotaa khyaal*-s—a difference of tempo.

The other varieties in the light-classsical category like *chaiti, kajari, saavani, jhoolaa, hori,* etc., differ in their themes only and, depending on the tempo, assume either a *thumri* or a *daadraa* character.

TAAL

Another interesting thing to note is that in general the *taal*-s employed in the *thumri-daadraa* family reflect a peculiar choice in their *theka-bol*-s. Every beat of the *taal* has one syllable.

For example:

1. *Taal Deepchandi* (14 beats)

1	2	3	4	5	6	7
dhaa	dhin	–	dhaa	dhaa	ti	–

8	9	10	11	12	13	14
ta	tin	–	dhaa	dhaa	dhin	–

2. *Taal Keherwaa* (8 beats)

1	2	3	4	5	6	7	8
dhaa	gi	na	ti	na	ka	dhi	na

3. *Taal Daadraa* (6 beats)

1	2	3	4	5	6
dhaa	dhi	na	dhaa	ti	naa

In these three *taal*-s, each beat has one syllable, the space between two beats is 'quiet'—without any syllable. To make this point clearer, in the *thekaa* of *Ektaal*, the word *'tirakita'* used for the fourth and the tenth beat is made up of 4 syllables *ti-ra-ki-ta*. This word occupies the whole space between the two beats fourth and fifth and again between the tenth and eleventh. *Taal*-s like *Rupak, Jhap taal, Teentaal* and even *Dhamaar*, which are common in classical forms, are also used for *thumri* compositions, and interestingly they too use one syllable for each beat of the *taal*.

1. *Taal Dhamaar* (14 beats)

1	2	3	4	5	6	7
ka	dhi	ta	dhi	ta	dhaa	–

8	9	10	11	12	13	14
ka	ti	ta	ti	ta	taa	–

2. *Taal Teentaal* (16 beats)

1	2	3	4	5	6	7	8
dhaa	dhin	dhin	dhaa	dhaa	dhin	dhin	dhaa

9	10	11	12	13	14	15	16
dhaa	tin	tin	taa	taa	dhin	dhin	dhaa

3. *Taal Jhap taal* (10 beats)

1	2	3	4	5	6	7	8	9	10
dhi	naa	dhi	dhi	naa	ti	naa	dhi	dhi	naa

4. *Taal Rupak* (7 beats)

1	2	3	4	5	6	7
ti	ti	naa	dhi	naa	dhi	naa

One syllable to a beat—this aspect of the *thekaa* may be allowing more freedom to the movement of the phrases and expression of the words in *bol-banaav*. It is also likely that because of this choice *Punjaabi taal* is rarely employed today for *thumri* texts and obviously rarely heard. Thus, barring a few *raag*-s and *taal*-s, *thumri* can make itself comfortable in many *raag*-s and *taal*-s that a pure classical abstract form - *khyaal* is using today. The easy transition of many *bol-baant thumri*-s into *chotaa khyaai*-s speaks of the vulnerable position of these two forms.

Enterprising musicians have composed *thumri-daadraa* songs in serious *raag*-s also and, even in light *raag*-s. Some of the new compositions exhibit a change in melodic contours.

USE OF PURE MUSICAL MATERIAL: AALAAP, TAAN AND SARGAM

Compared to the phrases with *bol*-s in which phrases get coloured with the literary meaning of the words, *aalaap, taan* and *sargam* are considered pure musical materials because they convey only musical meaning. Therefore, when *aalaap, taan,* and *sargam* enter *thumri* as decorative phrases, not only do they enchance the beauty of *thumri* but also add to its inherent abstract potential.

LAGGI

The *laagi* in the *tablaa* accompaniment had an important role in *thumri* when *thumri* was associated with dance. But even when *thumri* dissociated itself from dance, the *laggi* still accompanied *thumri* irrespective of the emotional content of the theme (even when the song was of separation, longing).The role *laggi* now played was to help *thumri* to evolve as a musical form independent of dance and the meaning of words. *Laggi* allowed fast melodic and rhythmic variations of the *mukhdaa* and produced a climatic musical excitement. The *laggi* added to the abstract character of *thumri* and continued as a musical need.

The freedom *thumri* enjoys today in respect of *raag, taal,* musical material, expression, treatment and development shows a new dimension of the form. The boundaries or limitations of a form need to be studied carefully in the context of changing times. Like *khyaal, thumri* also is adapting itself for survival. Its fight to mature towards a greater abstraction is really commendable. It is perhaps natural that all less abstract vocal art forms should aspire to the condition of *khyaal,* which represents the abstract vocal art form.

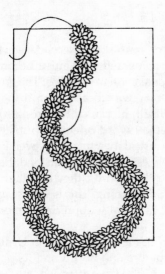

10

GHAZAL SINGING IN THE TWENTIETH CENTURY

We would never have believed that any non filmy musical form would equal the popularity of film music. But after seeing the crowded full-houses of *ghazal* concerts, and hearing *ghazal* tapes in every home, restaurant and car cassette player, we are forced to admit that the popularity of *ghazal* has equalled that of film music.

Film music became popular because it has musical qualities, very appealing to the laymen. In addition, its simple poetry is accompanied by visual of the film and the glamour of actors and actresses. It entices even the villagers with its commonly appealing elements.

Compared with film music, today's *ghazal* is much more complex. Its rhythm is far more difficult, the language sometimes is also not familiar. Yet *ghazal* has become very popular. Why?

Broadly speaking, there are two types of music—'*Swara* oriented' and 'word oriented'. *Swara* dominated music is generally connected with the concept of *raag* and word dominated music is connected with words and their emotional content. Therefore, it is easier to understand word dominated music. The listener enjoys music through poetry; music being secondary in this type of music. Words which are ornamented with music become more meaningful and their emotional content deepens. The words endow music with their own literary wealth and even if the listener does not understand music itself, he can still appreciate *ghazal* through its words. In fact, to enjoy word oriented forms it is not necessary to understand the musical meaning. However, in *swara* dominated music, it is absolutely essential to understand the musical meaning because even if there are words, they lose their identity in terms of tonal structure and meaning. This is why *swara* oriented music, i.e., classical music is usually appreciated more by knowledgeable listeners only.

As poetry, *ghazal* has a unique place in Urdu literature. It has its own specific structure and norms and its poetic content has a special quality. Those who have attended '*mushaairaa*-s' or '*shaairi*' programmes, or have seen them in films, may have noticed the audience's spontaneous participation in these events. After the poet or singer has sung half the stanza, the listeners complete the remaining part of it. From this excited exchange, one can appreciate the importance words have in *ghazal*. This is why *ghazal* comes under the category of word oriented music.

Ghazal began as a literary piece of work. When it entered the field of music it came under the influence of music itself. So much so, that music in *ghazal* has the upper hand today. *Ghazal* has completely changed with time. Its beginnings were marked by recitation of poetry only, but today its musical rendering draws from any type of music. In fact *ghazal* has come close even to *khyaal* which is at present the representative form of classical music.

Thumri, the light classical form took its place next to *khyaal* in the classical music concert quite recently. *Thumri* as sung by the courtesans was highly developed in terms of musical complexity. It had a definite tendency towards classical music due to its association with the *kalaavantin*. However, the *thumri* was not initially accepted in the classical concert. As times changed and society's outlook became more liberal, it gained acceptance next to *khyaal* on the classical platform. Music lovers who had kept away from classical music were readily able to respond to *thumri* because in its musical elaboration it gave importance to words. *Thumri* gradually incorporated the occasional use of *taan* and *sargam*. It did not try to compete however, with *khyaal*.

The *ghazal* of leading artists today, in contrast to the *thumri* is astonishingly flexible and commanding in character. It has borrowed a wide variety of elements from many music cultures of the world. Sometimes *ghazal* has a slow measured gait, and sometimes it cascades with very fast *taan*-s. It playfully dances with *sargam* and manipulates rhythm with such skill and dexterity, that one is amazed. It often assumes even the intoxicating thrill of disco rhythms. It has also incorporated the principle of chord progression in Western music and musical intervals hitherto unheard in Indian music. In duet singing, use of harmony or 'seconds' is also heard at times. The use of such ornamentation has added a more contemporary charm to its otherwise classical based structure.

At times *ghazal* also possesses the dignity and serenity of *khyaal*. When one listens to *ghazal* tunes, one can hardly believe to what extent it has stretched the concept of '*raag*'. Even in terms of accompaniment a single *haarmonium* or an orchestra are equally adaptable for the *ghazal*. Duet singing has lent it a new flavour adding to its popularity. In addition, *ghazal* has also achieved an attractive visual appearance.

The *ghazal* singers are equalling playback singers nay, surpassing them in the number of their concert engagements. The fees of *ghazal* singers are comparable to playback singers. In spite of the costly rate of tickets, it is often impossible to obtain seats at *ghazal* concerts. *Ghazal*-s are extremely popular outside India too. *Ghazal* singer's recordings can be found in almost every Indian household abroad. The effect of *ghazal* has stimulated resident Indians in the West to form their own groups, cut records and even come to India to give performances. Today *ghazal* has reached such a point of mass appeal that it may be composed and rendered in any way, still listeners will accept it. Such musical elements as *aalaap*, *taan* and *sargam* which are distinct features of classical music, when adopted to *ghazal* are quickly accepted by audiences and appreciated without any difficulty. Yet, when the same elements are offered on the platter of classical music, the same audience says, "Oh! We don't understand anything!" and they stay away from classical music. Classical musicians must search for the reason why such listeners are not attracted to classical music. A distinct feature of *ghazal* today is its flexible form which offers endless variety and possibilities. Some of the noteworthy features of *ghazal* are its unique combination of notes and phrases, its richness and variety in expression, its lively *'thekaa'* and the *'tihaai-s'* as in classical music, its playful sport with *'laya'*, its clear and emotional enunciation of words, its tonal qualities rounded, broad, husky, heavy and still very supple, its ample use of different tonal textures, its easy and tuneful use of all three octaves, its difficult, well-designed and colourful acrobatics.

Like the beauty of neatly drawn *rangoli, ghazal* immediately enchants every one. From the foregoing, it may be appreciated that singing *ghazal*-s is not an easy task. Even those who have mastered classical music must think twice before venturing to enter the path along which noted artists have developed the *ghazal*.

A new style of playing the *haarmonium* in accordance with the *ghazal* has also been developed. The voice runs after the imagination, and the fingers on the *haarmonium* after the voice. *Ghazal* singers are usually excellent *haarmonium* players. The coordination between the voice, *haarmonium* and *tablaa* is remarkable. *Tablaa* players accompanying *ghazal* singers constitute a class of their own. They require special training. It is a very difficult thing to sing the *mukhdaa* of *ghazal* with *laggi* on the *tablaa*.

One cannot tell whether or not *ghazal* will affect classical music.

Khyaal has been equally open and flexible. This has not only protected its existence but also given it the principal place in classical music today. Will *'khyaal'* need to change to protect itself from the potential of *'ghazal'*? Will *'ghazal'* take a place next to *'khyaal'* as did *'thumri'* and gain acceptance in classical concerts? The answer to these questions depends upon us, the listeners.

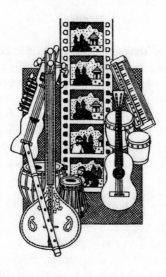

11

FILM MUSIC - ORCHESTRA PROGRAMMES

I am a classical musician, but film music has always appealed to me. It has made me think differently, and has given me new insights. Secondly, film music has been constantly pointed out as the greatest competitor/enemy of classical music. This is also the reason why I felt the need to know more about film music—what is so special about this music which has completely enamoured the common man.

Today's film music not only embraces everything from folk to classical music in India, but also opens up for all types of music and instruments from other countries. It has borrowed anything from anywhere that appealed to it, digested it and put its own stamp on it. Strangely it did not leave even Western harmony which is considered harmful to melody—the soul of Indian music. It would not be wrong to say that film music has given birth to a new harmony with Indian soul. Because of the use of this harmony, the so called knowledgeables regarded film music as non-Indian music. Funnily Western musicians never laid claims on this harmony. Attired differently and sporting a new look, this Indian harmony provided a strong foundation, backdrop to film music.

It was no wonder that the main melodic contour stood out prominently dazzling with its features against the dense backdrop of the Indian harmony. At times, however, this harmony became irritating, redundant and also overpowering. But the fault lies with the composer. A judicious use of harmony has now become a distinctive feature of Indian film music.

Film music has captured the masses through its simple tunes which anybody can hum, attractive rhythms and easy to understand lyrics. Besides, the story and picture background have contributed in increasing its popularity. Today, if one were to ask which type of music is dear to all Indians, the answer would undoubtedly be film music. Viewed from this perspective film music could be termed as mass music.

Very often film music is derogatorily referred to as frivolous music. This viewpoint is largely substantiated due to the stubborn attitude of the critics who have obviously not heard enough film music and have not bothered to study it in depth. They don't realise that they are doing great injustice to film music out of their half-baked knowledge and prejudices.

Every music has its own grammar, discipline and technique as does film music. If one were to take to playback singing it wouldn't be that easy. Even a well-trained classical musician would have to think a hundred times before facing a microphone. Though film music may be light on the ears, its technique is far from simple.

Film music has oriented new possibilities in the field of Indian music. While evolving itself it has enriched other forms of music as well. It has forced the listener to think about various aspects of music differently. It has shown new directions. Playback singers like Lata Mangeshkar, Asha Bhosle, Kishore Kumar, Mohammad Rafi, etc., have set new standards in throw of voice, sweetness, roundness of tone, tonal variations, range, expressions, ease, polish, precision, beauty, clarity, variety, enunciation of words, etc.

The skills and talents of composers, instrumentalists, singers and recording technicians are complete in themselves and their synchronisation ensures perfection of every moment of the song which emerges 'perfect' in every respect. The effect of such a song is also perfect. Although the actual song is of 4-5 minutes, a lot of thinking, energy, effort and time are expended on it. Since only the 'best' is presented in the song, the competition in this field has reached its peak.

The other distinctive feature of film music is its rhythm. In public concerts and on TV, one sees a variety of instruments used for rhythm—even an unconventional material is used effectively as rhythm instrument. Innovative musicians have brought in unthinkable variety in rhythmic patterns and their expression.

Often film and classical music are compared for no reason.There is a continuous brain washing by putting classical music on a higher pedestal. Why this attempt to mislead people? No form of music is superior or inferior. It can only be good or bad. It is mainly the talent and ability of the artist which make the music he represents good or bad. Is it fair to say that Lata, Asha's music is inferior because they have chosen film medium. Similarly, if a classical musician is singing off-tune, off-beat and dry, will it be fair to call his music superior just because it belongs to the classical genre? Many film songs are based on pure *raag*-s. If such songs are included in the repertoire of a classical concert, what is wrong? *Naatya sangeet* (theatre songs) having classical base is accepted in a concert, why not *raag* based film songs? One must do away with preconceived notions and approach any music with open mind. Only then can we be called ourselves connoisseurs in the true sense.

Just a few years ago, a music concert meant mainly a classical music concert. But now, almost all forms of music—*naatya sangeet*, *ghazal*-s, *bhajan*-s, even film songs are presented in public concerts in different catchy styles with impressive visuals. Amongst these forms, film music based shows which came to be known as orchestra-shows have gained tremendous popularity. Daily one comes across atleast one such advertisement of an orchestra programme in the leading newspapers. But sadly, these programmes have not gained the expected respectability. On account of purely commercial approach, the standards of these programmes have reached low levels. Their only object being to gain popularity and earn money, a lot of cheap gimmicks besides music have crept in. Respectable cultured people have preferred to stay away from these programmes. Such orchestra programmes have further harmed the outlook of the society towards film music which was already put into a low caste category.

The only rewarding factor is that several promising young artists involved in these programmes got the opportunity to present their talent before the public. They received encouragement, fame and money and most important got a chance to better their art. Learning music is getting more and more expensive. Orchestra programmes provided financial assistance.

The standard of film music will improve only when a listener of film music will start differentiating between good and bad film music. Only then will he turn to classical music. One must realise how important it is to include all musical genres (forms) besides the classical in music education.

12

MUSIC MAKERS

In any performing art, actual performance is the ultimate goal and that is why artists become very important. They are always in the limelight; they are placed on a higher pedestal than others. Sadly, people like *guru*-s and theoreticians and in modern times, newspaper critics who are directly or indirectly responsible for training, nurturing, moulding and projecting artists, often remain in the background, unnoticed, even ignored. Very often their role in the evolution and development of art is underestimated and misjudged. The *guru*-s keep art traditions alive by imparting training and sharing their knowledge and experience. The scholars formulate theories on the basis of critical analysis of various performances in the context of material, content, structure, styles, and trends. They thus provide a fund of reference to the artists for their presentations and to the critics for evaluating such presentations.

Another important constituent of performing arts that has been ignored again and again is the listener-viewer. Can performing arts survive without them? During its long history, performing arts have continuously shaped themselves according to the demands of the listener-viewers. The encouragement an artist receives from the listener-viewer in actual performance inspires him and takes him to greater heights. Apart from anything else, it is the degree of rapport between a sensitive performer and discerning listener-viewer which decides the success of any performance. Has anything been done for training listener-viewer? Is it not necessary to raise the standard of our listener-viewer?

By offering a professional stage to the performers and exposing masses to live performances, cultural organizations have indirectly trained the masses in the appreciation of art.

Let us understand that performers and listener-viewers, *guru*-s and academicians, organisers and critics all have their role to play in the creation and development of performing arts.

I would like to draw your attention to one more thing. We have certain traditional biases towards popular music. By popular music I mean film music, pop music, *ghazal*-s, etc. Is it not wrong on our part to compare classical music with popular music? Popular music needs to be appreciated in its own context. The norms for judging music of Lata Mangeshkar and Mehdi Hassan cannot be the same as in classical music. There are good performers and bad performers in all kinds of music. Music in itself cannot be good or bad; the artist makes it good or bad. We must understand that popular music in itself is not cheap.

Popularizing classical music and raising its standard have to go together. Perhaps we have been wrongly expecting everybody to take to classical music which was not only impractical but also destructive to classical music itself. Individuals come from different backgrounds and they also differ in their abilities. It is difficult to say which type of music will have a moving effect on a particular individual. Secondly, I am sure we do not want only classical music to survive. Different types of music are the natural expressions of various sections of society. There has been a lot of give and take between various types of music including classical. This mutual dependence is the necessity of each type of music for novelty, freshness, vigour, and sustenance. And that is why each type of music has to be nurtured carefully and consciously. Let us understand that classical music cannot live in isolation. We have to seriously think of promoting other lighter varieties such as film music, theatre music, light music and also folk music - which is the fountainhead of all human activity and emotions. Our concern should be for good music and not for the type of music. It is disheartening to see that a commercial element has entered even into classical arts. The commercial aspect which is dominating today's music festivals is the root cause of that 'cheap' thing whether it is classical or popular music. What measures are we taking to check these tendencies? The only answer I can think of is the conscious initiated listener. I strongly feel that cultural organizations must become centres of educational movement also. Otherwise, their activities will remain meaningless.

We are living in the age of science and technology. They have penetrated into every field of human activity. Even arts have not been able to stay away from their influence. The tremendous variety that has percolated from different corners of the world has opened new paths for thought, action and experience. Needless to stay that in performing arts, all scientific and theoretical issues, at the end, are tested on the platform in the actual performance.

The study of performing arts in different contexts, in their dimension of mutual interdependence has today become possible because of science and technology. The traditional teaching and learning processes are being supplemented by new techniques. This study has also accelerated the promotion, preservation and propagation of arts. It is the need of the time that the cultural, educational and commercial organizations come together and work for mutual benefit.

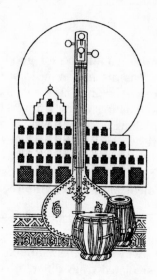

13

TEACHING MUSIC AT INSTITUTIONS

MY ORIENTATION

Music is essentially a performing art. Hence my approach to music education, private or institutional, has a significant bias towards competency in performance. I am aware that music is not only performance, it is a science as well. But what I mean by being biased towards performance is that all other aspects of music need to be studied in the context of performance. In other words, whether it is the acoustics of sound or the history of musical forms, whether it is the psychology or sociology of music or the anatomy of the voice, every aspect of music under study must have relevance to actual 'contemporary' performance. Ultimately, all the scientific and theoretical issues should converge on and be tested upon the concert platform of 'today'. They should contribute towards enriching the musical performance itself.

I am a product of *'guru-shishya paramparaa'*. I have been teaching music privately for many years and I have also taught for 13 years in an institutional framework. I find that both the systems lack something because they take a singular approach. In *guru-shishya* system, the accent is on the performance, while in the institutional system, the stress is on the academic study of music. Even then, everybody who is trained in *guru-shishya* system, doesn't become a performer in the real sense. Similarly every research student who is groomed for Ph.D. award doesn't become a Doctor of Music in the real sense.

Here, I shall speak mainly about my experience and ideas concerning the teaching of music in institutions. I believe that in the days to come, more and more institutions will become the centres of teaching music on a mass scale. But before discussing the curricula, methods, teaching aids, etc., I feel it is necessary to dwell upon the objectives we want to achieve and to review the problems already existing in music education. Without deciding upon objectives and surveying the facilities presently available to achieve them, any discussion of institutional music education is pointless.

The first question I think we must answer is why should there be music education at all? In general, the feeling is that music is a source of diversion, an amusement to while away the hours of leisure. In a sense this is true. Music is not included among those essentials of life such as food, clothing and shelter. Even so, we know that since time immemorial music has been an integral part of life! We have seen that during prayer, in the task of mitigating the burden of physical labour, in satisfying the urge for emotional and creative expression, music has played a principal role for centuries. Gifted with the ability to apprehend the beautiful, man's creative instinct found its expression in art. Music earned the highest place of honour among the arts, for it did not depend on any visual or tactile object to express itself.

When music came to exist for its own sake, it flowered into a form of art which came to be used for entertainment. In today's world, music is the most popular and widespread form of entertainment available to the common man.

But what about the great potential that music has in the formation of human character? Plato has said, "Musical training is a more potent instrument than any other because, rhythm and harmony find their way into the inward places of the soul". Isn't music a symbol of harmony and balance? When we realize the truth behind this, we recognize the existence of a kind of music beyond our usual concept of music. This music is merged in the whole universe and every single object in creation reflects it in terms of harmony, balance and beauty. When we begin to perceive this deeper and more subtle meaning of music, we realise how music is capable of bringing harmony and balance into human life and how essential music is for meaningful human existence.

It is in this context also that we have to evaluate our present system of music education. Mere existence is not life. Only when existence is meaningful and consistent can we describe it as life. This transformation can be achieved only through meaningful education. Socrates has described education as "Kindling of a flame; not filling of an empty vessel". We need to evaluate our present education in the light of this definition. Does it enrich the character and personality of our students? In my view, our present system encourages accumulation of facts and figures. The objectives of developing analytical and critical skills, artistic and aesthetic sensibilities, and balanced and healthy minds capable of facing life with understanding and humility are largely neglected.

What I would like to point out and underline, however, is that the very attitudes that we possess towards the place of music in life, invariably influence the objectives we set for ourselves and the methods we use to achieve them. As long as we are unable to keep in constant view, the fact that music is a suitable and powerful force in shaping the society and social values, we shall not be able to treat it with the seriousness, respect and responsibility that it rightly deserves.

OBJECTIVES

In our discussion of objectives, we have to take into consideration certain traditional biases that have deeply affected our aims and scope of music education. Generally, when we think of music education or music appreciation, we have in mind only classical music. Somehow nobody deems it necessary to think of folk music, light music, film or pop music in the context of music education. We seem to be convinced that music forms such as *bhajan*-s, *ghazal*-s, film or folk songs can be appreciated, understood and learnt without much effort. We are reluctant to admit film music or *ghazal*-s into our curriculum because these musical forms have been traditionally scorned upon as easy, uncultivated and cheap. This situation prevails in spite of the fact that today's education is meant for the masses and the preference of the masses is for popular music—light music, film music.

Such biases need to be seriously re-examined in the context of the music of such masters as Begam Akhtar, Mehdi Hassan, Ghulam Ali, Lata Mangeshkar, Asha Bhosle, Kishore Kumar, and Mohammad Rafi, to name just a few great *ghazal* and playback singers. The music of these musicians reflects a sound classical base, training and expertise, but they have chosen to use it for light and film music rather than for classical. Since light music is so popular and since it also draws richly from elements used in classical music, why don't we exploit the situation and include *ghazal* and film music in our curriculum? Why don't we take the opportunity to make our students aware of the 'good' and 'bad' in this music and thereby expose them to the basic principles of music? Through these light forms, they will also realise the worth of classical music and will gradually be led to classical music itself. In addition, this will enhance their respect for classical music and develop their taste in the field. Today's music education should therefore aim at being all inclusive. It should be able to teach *khyaal*, *thumri* or even folk or film songs without preconceived notions. The primary objective throughout should be a high standard of performance in all types of forms, because it is only this that will enrich both science or '*shastra*' and art of music.

Unfortunately, when theory is dealt with in our institutions, it is usually concerned with what is written in our ancient treatises on music or it perpetuates our myths and legends about music and musicians of the past. Very little of this theory is relevant to actual contemporary performance. Perhaps this is why musicians normally scoff at musicologists. The latter's knowledge of theory and history often has little bearing upon performance itself. This chasm dividing the performer and the scholar needs to be overcome through an attempt to concentrate on the issues that directly enhance performance. One needs to remember that inevitably there is a gap between theory and practice. Performance always precedes theoretical principles. Even historically, it seems reasonable to expect that music first developed its own form and complexity and then, only later, did it get embodied and codified in theoretical concepts. At a given time, one particular theory could not possibly assimilate and reflect all the experiments and changes that followed. Therefore, when we consider what aspects of musical theory we need to include in our curriculum today, our criteria should be how relevant it is to contemporary performance. Failing this, theory is bound to be dry and inert.

Besides theory, it is worth asking why music institutions have not considered introducing specialized training in the many professional areas related to music. As we know, musical activity involves not only performance of various types of music from classical to film music, but also organisers, listeners, critics, teachers, writers, composers, instrument makers, audio-technicians, CD and cassette dealers, manufacturers of audio equipment and so on. On the science side, music is also related to other disciplines like psychology, sociology, acoustics, philosophy, religion, poetry, etc. Music is applied in areas such as physical exercise or aerobics, medical therapy, psychotherapy, plant therapy, etc. For each of these professions and specialised areas, a highly specialised training is necessary in addition to basic competence in performing and analysing music. If music education offered a wider choice of activity and was job-oriented, more people would get involved with music as a serious endeavour. In highlighting professional options for students in the field of music, it would also change the prevalent conception about music as merely a means of entertainment. With the economic pressures of modern living, this kind of orientation would provide economic incentive to persue a musical vocation.

PRESENT STATE OF AFFAIRS - SOME PROBLEMS

If we accept the foregoing as some of our principal objectives, can we hope to achieve them under the present conditions at music institutions? What are some of the major problems that we face at present? First of all, any institution's reputation is based upon its administration and the quality of its faculty members. The most important teaching tool in education is the teacher himself. All other tools depend on him and they cannot replace him but only supplement him. Do we have sufficiently competent teachers in our music institutions? What do I mean by competence? I mean firstly a certain standing in musical performance. The reason I stress this requirement is because music is basically a performing art and should therefore be taught by those who themselves know how to perform. One of the most fundamental drawbacks in institutions, is that students cannot hope to receive instruction from the masters and veterans who command the professional field. For this level of training, they have to seek private instruction from artists of their choice.

At this point, it is well worth considering why there are very few professional performers teaching at music institutions. One of the reasons is that the status of music teachers is not much respected. The salary scale of educators is also appalling, compared to the fees of star musicians. A performer would never be inclined to teach at an institution for reasons of income. Secondly, he would not think of getting involved in music institutions unless he had a keen interest in academic study which is directly related to contemporary performance. Another reason is that institutions themselves do not offer professional platform which is essential to maintain quality in performance; they also tend to control and restrict their teacher's movements, something that would be suicidal for the professional skill and career of a musician. In music education, public performance must be treated as a part and parcel of the teaching profession and leave of absence should be granted as a right and not as a special concession. One objection to this is that if a teacher is allowed to keep up his concert engagements throughout the year, he would rarely be present for his teaching commitments. This is not altogether true. Concerts are held usually on week-ends and a performer who is committed to teaching would certainly try to make adjustments between the two and strike a balance. A musician retired from the performing field would be ideally suited for teaching. To my mind, performance, teaching and academic research should all be interlinked.

One way of exposing students to artists of repute is by inviting them to teach during their least busy season for a month or two. Something like an artist-in-residence scheme would be a rare opportunity for students to learn under masters. Normally, no artist would permit any one near him while he is practising, but in an institution, he may permit the students to hear him practice. Listening to a performer's *'riyaz'* would help the students learn how and what to practice to achieve skill in performance.

Similarly, teachers should also be sent to different institutions for a term-in-residence for exposure to new environments and for exchange of ideas. Institutions could take advantage of the presence of teachers from other parts of the country who may have special areas of interest and proficiency to share with the students. Besides competence in performance, another equally important prerequisite for teachers in institutions is their efficiency in dealing with the theoretical aspect of music. A major setback of the *guru-shishya paramparaa* system is that students are rarely exposed to critical thinking in terms of performance and its various aspects. By theory I mean any subject related to music such as psycho-acoustics, voice-culture, aesthetics, etc. As such, the traditional method has little scope for a scientific approach to learning music. This is possibly one reason why the *guru-shishya paramparaa* system is so time consuming and tedious. With better scientific methods, a student may be able to progress faster even in an institution, if he is given in addition; practical systematic exercises, access to the necessary technological aids such as tape-recorders, studios, laboratories and so on. Relevant theory would go a long way in accelerating a student's progress.

The responsibility of making theory useful and meaningful would rest upon the teacher. Unfortunately, the teachers of today lack such an orientation and it is seldom that one comes across a teacher who is aware and proficient at both performance and its theoretical dimensions. I have a suggestion that theory papers should be taught by visiting faculty.

Sometimes a teacher may be a good performer and an intelligent theoretician, but he may not possess the right skills required for teaching. Under the circumstances, an institute for training competent music personnel is urgently required. Ironically, it is sufficient to possess any music certificate to gain a position as teacher.

It is necessary for teachers also to undergo a periodic assessment of their contribution and standard in the Department. Unlike in the West, where teachers are enthusiastically engaged in constantly thinking about their subject in new and stimulating ways, teachers in India are generally very apathetic and indifferent. Besides teaching, if they hold extra-curricular activities at the class and department level like seminars and workshops, or supervise the publication of a magazine which includes articles written by students and teachers, this would totally alter the learning atmosphere and it would be re-energised and would promote the growth of a music department or institution. It is really ironic that when teachers are asked to attend workshops, seminars, performances, competitions or other related activities during the weekend, they are reluctant and expect time off during the week to recover their time lost. They are not open and willing to try new methods nor to explore new areas. A competent teacher with a broad vision is a basic necessity of the music institutions. If our own teachers cannot set a good example, how can we ever expect our students to be more interested and hard working?

A good rapport between students and teachers is an important factor in creating interest and accelerating the learning process. This can happen only if teachers take the initiative to organize activities that would bring the two together. At the same time, a dialogue between the commercial music world outside and music institutions is also very necessary. Teachers should keep regular contacts with experts outside and try to organize lecture-demonstrations and workshops with the help of students and faculty members. Special concessions and deals from organizers for attending their concerts, would also expose students to the professional world.

Another problem of fundamental importance in our institutions is the lack of appropriate resources such as well-stocked libraries of music books and recordings. There is hardly any material readily available on specific topics related to music that may be recommended as text-books and references for the students. Such specialised material needs to be prepared and translated into various regional languages. A list of the topics of Ph.D. students working in various institutions should be sent to a central place for compilation and circulation. This way students can keep abreast of all the specialised research work available and going on in the field.

Modern technological aids such as music studios, laboratories with listening facilities, practice rooms with instruments, *tablaa* accompaniment and supervisors for practice sessions, recital or concert halls, TVs, videos and radios would all make a significant contribution to the student's exposure and development. If a student habitually taped his practice and analysed it with his peers, it would help him appraise himself objectively and also encourage him to become self-sufficient and independent.

The availability of such aids depends on funding. Since the government does not subsidize music departments, funding depends on the number of students enrolled in the department. Even at the college level, since music is not treated at par with other subjects, the allotment of funds is meagre. The consequences of having to depend upon the number of students enrolled in a department, even for its continuity are that, entrance requirements are very lax, expectations from students are very low and assessment of quality is arbitrary and routine. These conditions lead to a decline in standards and it is a sad fact that the students who obtain their degrees and certificates thereby, use them as proofs of their competence for obtaining jobs and for their self importance. It goes without saying that in the world of performance, these paper qualifications have little meaning and that the real test is always the practical demonstration of skill. Unless these institutions upgrade their staff, establish higher standards and restrict awarding their certificates to only those who deserve them, these degrees will remain meaningless and questionable in the commercial world of performance. This is one of the reasons why there is such a wide gap between the commercial world of performance and the institutional world of music teaching. Until our educational institutions themselves become centres of cultural movement and interact with the commercial world of music, music education in institutions will remain meaningless. Its involvement with the competitive world outside is essential. Through this contact, the evaluation of the staff and students by the institution and by the commercial world will occur simultaneously and the quality of performance of students will automatically be raised.

Syllabus and Methods

Keeping in mind this background and the objectives enumerated earlier, let me now address the question of methods in teaching music. The first step would be the overall formation and planning of a syllabus that begins right from the kindergarten level to graduation. The specific contents of a syllabus at every level and the aids available would directly influence the methods required for teaching that material. By the time a student reaches graduation, he should have achieved a basic standard of competence in performance and should have studied music in relation to various scientific and theoretical areas. He should be sufficiently prepared to undertake post-graduate work in areas of specialisation such as cultural history, aesthetics, philosophy, sociology, and psychology of music or different types of music like folk, light, temple, theatre, film, Karnatak, Western, World music, or instrumental, choral and orchestral music, etc.

Standardisation of basic materials to be taught both in performance and theory is necessary because certain skills and concepts are fundamental for every student. Whether it is in vocal or instrumental music, the awareness of correct pitch, tonal colour and rhythm, the consciousness of the subtle movements of the notes and their notational values, beauty, balance, clarity in presentation and the knowledge of the various characteristics of *raag*-s and *taal*-s and the peculiarities of different musical forms, like *khyaal, thumri, bhajan,* etc., should all be developed.

A standard exercise book containing note-exercises of different patterns (solfaggios) in simple *raag*-s should be prepared as in Karnatak music. This way the student could collect in his memory a store of note-patterns, develop dexterity and ease in rendering notes in any given combinations and gain basic technical skills in the use of his voice and instrument. The *'merukhand'* system teaches how to create a variety of patterns with a given number of notes by changing their content in terms of the position of a note in a pattern, its duration and expression. Both the standard note-exercises and the *merukhand* system should be applied together. This will help students improvise and think creatively in the context of a *raag* and form.

In this respect the role of *sargam* or notation is very important. It enables a student to become conscious of his own musical activity. The practice of various note-patterns in the five vowels *aa, e, i, o, u* would develop purity of vowel tone at any pitch.

It must also be stressed that basic exercises must be practised throughout the student's career, for it is only over a long period that his technique will get polished and his knowledge and expression will gain depth and maturity. The *raag*-s - *Kalyaan* and *Bhairavi* are ideal especially during the early years of training because they accustom the student to all the twelve notes in the Indian scale. Students should be taught compositions in different musical forms such as *khyaal, taraanaa, thumri, daadraa, tappaa, bhajan* in the same *raag* so that they come to know how, given the same scale, note-combinations and their expressions change according to the musical form; that is what we call 'application' of music.

The student should also be taught an instrument if one is a vocalist and singing if one is an instrumentalist. This will help reinforce learning and perceptual understanding. Learning *veenaa* or *saarangi* would help a vocalist appreciate the movements of notes such as *'meend*-s' and *'gamak*-s'. Likewise, a *sitaar* player would benefit in lending emotional colour to his music while playing if he knew vocal music, as most instrumental music is based upon vocal music.

Using simple and attractive words and themes relevant to the present times and different age groups, songs should be composed in different *raag*-s. One of the reasons for the popularity of film and light music is its word content. In addition to specially written songs, we can easily draw from our rich *bhakti* literature in various dialects for this purpose.

While learning song-text—

1. Students should first practice reading the text aloud many times for correct pronunciation and understanding its meaning.
2. The composition should first be practised in *sargam* so that its musical structure and overall form becomes clear.
3. The same composition then should be sung using only *'aa'* vowel.
4. The composition later on should be sung using *thekaa-bol*-s to understand its *taal* structure.
5. And lastly comes singing song-text with words.

Raag Kalyaan
Taal Jhap taal

Song-text

Sthaayi
Mana sumira shree Ganesha
Mangala naam

Antaraa
Vidyaa guna daataa
Hota mangala kaam

Beat position:

1	2	3	4	5	6	7	8	9	10

Sargam:

N	P	R	R	S	Ṇ	R	G	–	G

Thekaa-bol-s:

dhi	naa	dhi	dhi	naa	ti	naa	dhi	dhi	naa

Vowel '*aa*':

aa	–	–	–	–	–	–	–	–	–

Words of the first line:

Ma	na	su	mi	ra	shree	Ga	ne	–	sha

The individual beats of the *taal* should be counted simultane-ously by hand showing its characteristic pattern through claps and wave.

To develop the ability of keeping *taal* and improvising in the context of different rhythmic cycles and tempi, the student should be made to practice *taal* oriented note-patterns that fit into different *taal* structures.

For example:

For *Jhap taal* of 10 beats, the exercises could be -

1. Single note

1	2	3	4	5	6	7	8	9	10
dhi	naa	dhi	dhi	naa	ti	naa	dhi	dhi	naa
S	R	S	R	G	R	G	R	G	M etc.

2. To double it:

1	2	3	4	5
Ṣ R	S R	G R	G R	G M

etc., repeated twice.

3. To triple it:

1	2	3	4	5
S R S	R G R	G R G	M S R	S R G

etc., repeated thrice.

4. To quadruple it:

1	2	3	4	5
S R S R	G R G R	G M S R	S R G R	G R G M

etc., repeated four times.

For other *taal*-s same method can be applied—there can be a variety of note-patterns corresponding to the *thekaa* and divisions of the *taal*.

Ektaal (12 beats)

	1	2	3	4	5	6
	dhin	*dhin*	*dhaage*	*tirakita*	*tu*	*naa*
(i)	S	R	⌊G M⌋	⌊P D N Ṡ⌋	N	Ṡ
(ii)	S	R	⌊S R⌋	⌊S R G M⌋	P	D

	7	8	9	10	11	12
	kat	*taa*	*dhaage*	*tirakita*	*dhi*	*naa*
(i)	Ṡ	N	⌊Ṡ N⌋	⌊D P M G⌋	R	S
(ii)	N	Ṡ	⌊Ṡ N⌋	⌊D P M G⌋	R	S

Students should be asked to make their own patterns from simple to complex and demonstrate their skills in performing them at various tempi. This would be both a stimulating, challenging, and if well done, a satisfying experience for the students. Just as *sitaar* players learn *tablaa* compositions and compose musical phrases based on them, vocalists should also learn similar compositions to apply them in constructing vocal phrases. The skill of playing basic *thekaa*-s of *taal*-s on the *tablaa* should be compulsory. It would enhance the student's sense of rhythmic patterns and increase his understanding of the role of rhythm in Indian music.

The importance of practice cannot be stressed enough. Institutional teaching leaves the responsibility of sufficient practice to the student himself. One of the great advantages in the *guru-shishya paramparaa* system was that the *guru* demanded long hours of sustained practice from his students, often under his own supervision. I think institutions should not leave it to the students to practise as and when they wish. They should be required to spend a certain amount of time everyday practising in the premises of the institution preferably under supervision. Attendance for these practice sessions should be made mandatory and some percentage of the final marks should be allotted to it. The use of tape-recorders during practice should be encouraged. If the student listened to his own practice, he would learn to be more objective, critical and self-appraising with reference to his playing or singing. At times, when the teacher-supervisor cannot be present to hear and personally monitor the student's practice, the tape-recorder is a great boon and could act as an important self-corrective. If students listen to their recordings with fellow-students, they can exchange their views and thus develop communication skills and an open mind.

Another method of encouraging students to pay sufficient attention to their practice is through inter-collegiate exchange and competitions. This would give students an opportunity to perform before audiences and overcome their self-consciousness as well as appreciate the factors involved in performance itself. These competitions play a significant role in supporting those students who have talent and promise. Good students should also be made to participate in respectable public competitions that are held from time to time. Not only will this encourage them and make them bold, but it will bring credit to their institutions if they are successful and attract more students to it. These activities should be well publicized through the media.

The involvement of the press and other media like TV, radio with educational activities is important to promote education and culture.

An extremely critical aspect of music education is the development of the analytical ability by making theory of practical value. If a student happens to be studying the anatomy of voice, his study should help him achieve better tonal colour, better range, greater stamina and ease in his singing. If he happens to be studying the acoustics of sound, it should contribute towards his acquisition of a keener sense of the upper partials in his instrument or voice and an insight into the effect that the shape of a hall has upon the texture of the sound produced. If he is studying the history of classical music, he should be able to critically assess and describe the difference between the music of old masters in the context of their times through recordings that are available. The student's ability to speak and write about different aspects of music could be developed by holding seminars wherein they are required to present papers on topics of their choice. This would also create an atmosphere of discussion and exchange and stimulate their thinking.

In this connection, the ability to listen is perhaps the most essential tool a student needs in order to develop a mature musical understanding. Just as practice should be made mandatory, so also critical listening, descriptive evaluation, minute notation and even imitation of recordings should be made compulsory. The ability to notate is extremely important for the recognition of development and organization of a particular musical form or composition. Traditionally, notation was not regarded as relevant and helpful for students because it was felt that notation firstly, would prevent the student from memorizing what he learnt and secondly, that notation is incapable of capturing the subtle nuances of music. This has some truth in it. But those who are familiar with Western music and its notational system will know that the West has been able to capture the movement of sound to a remarkably sophisticated degree in their notational system. Unfortunately our attitude towards notation has always been so negative that it has restricted the development of an appropriate system of notation for Indian music. This powerful tool in the understanding of music needs to be given more attention.

Also related to the critical analysis of music is the development of appropriate technical terminology. It is a curious fact to note that the descriptive terminology for musical performance is being generated by a class of writers self-qualified to be 'music critics'. The ability to speak on music in specific terms so that the item being referred to is understood clearly by all those concerned with music reflects a certain level of sophistication in the intellectual development of that field. It is unfortunate that we have developed very little terminology in the context of contemporary performance beyond the pioneering work attempted by a few like V. N. Bhatkhande. Various Indian and Western authors have written on Indian music and have used several terms to describe a particular musical concept, but it is difficult to find a consistent and exact vocabulary of technical terms that North Indian musicians could commonly use and understand.

It is no wonder that if we ourselves are not able to communicate specific meaning when we discuss music, our students should also find it impossible to be expressively critical. I have been reading music reviews for over two decades and I am constantly amazed and even troubled by the fact that most often, readers of music-reviews are fed with more flowery rather than technically accurate descriptions of musical performance. The reason why this is of concern to me is that these music critics, who often have very little or no practical experience in music, are extremely powerful instruments in the education and moulding of the mass response to music. If a layman who has no musical understanding reads a review of a concert he had recently attended, the review would invariably influence his understanding and his future response to music.

CONCLUDING

Considering all the problems that exist at present, it may be far-fetched to expect institutions to come up with performers and theoreticians with considerable merit. However, it is definitely within their grasp to raise the standard of their student's understanding and judgement of music. Today it is the masses that patronize and hence control almost all musical activity. The only way to maintain a high level of quality in these avenues of public appearance is by raising the level of expectation of the listeners. If the audience were discerning of and sensitive to good quality, it would provide the necessary checks and balances required to maintain a reasonably high level of performance quality. Moreover, it is only a good listener who can eventually become a good performer. It is only he who would also contribute to other fields related to music. Therefore, let us start our music education with an attempt to at least nurture good listeners who will eventually persue music either as a profession or in its various related fields of endeavour.

14

STUDYING AND TEACHING AT THE UNIVERSITY OF CALIFORNIA, LOS ANGELES, USA

During my various concert tours abroad, whenever I performed or gave lecture-demonstrations, I realized that knowledge of the local musical traditions would have helped me describe Indian music in terms familiar to my audiences. I also observed that a new global view of music was emerging in which music of different cultures was being brought together. In response to this global music consciousness, most music faculties in the West established centres for World music at their universities to promote the exchange of skills and knowledge between cultures of the world.

ETHNOMUSICOLOGY

Ethnomusicology is a relatively new field which covers an exceptionally wide range of interdisciplinary subjects related to music. As a scientific discipline it attempts to obtain an overview of World music which is at once universal and culture specific. It uses field research and methods which include questionnaires, interviews, field recordings, classification systems, analysis and so on. It also deals with the issues of how to write and describe music in both visual and verbal terms.

PURPOSE OF THE VISIT

As an advisor and examiner for Ph.D. work, I constantly feel that most students in India lack scientific training in methods of research and analysis and that they are limited in their experience of the diversity in music because of the exclusive emphasis on Indian music. Exposure to creative inquiry and appropriate research methodologies have become essential for any music student today to be able to appreciate his own music, the music of various cultures and the changes that take place when different music cultures come in contact with each other. My purpose for applying for a Senior Fulbright Fellowship or the Indo-American Grant was thus motivated by a strong desire to study other cultures of music for my own enrichment, also to expand the music curriculum at the SNDT University where I was a professor and Head of the Department of Music. I decided to go to the University of California, Los Angeles since it had the largest programme in Ethnomusicology at that time in North America.

UCLA MUSIC DEPARTMENT

I found the Music Department at UCLA very impressive. Its facilities included sophisticated audio-visual equipment such as video, audio and disc-recorders, slide and film projectors, duplicators and computers, as well as a special laboratory for repairing instruments and equipment. The students and staff had easy access to the above facilities and were encouraged and specially trained in how to use them.

ETHNOMUSICOLOGY DEPARTMENT

The Ethnomusicology Department had scholars and specialists in such diverse areas as Africa, Middle East, South-East Asia, Europe and America and many of these areas had visiting artists or artists-in-residence such as myself to teach performance courses. In addition, guest lecturers who spoke and gave demonstration on their music specialization were a constant feature of the programme. I had an opportunity to meet the faculty and artists-in-residence and discuss with them on subjects of mutual interest. The librarian of the Ethnomusicology Archive, the largest of its kind in the United States, also agreed to keep in touch and suggest reading materials and recordings as and when they would be available.

AUDITING COURSES

During my three months stay in Los Angeles, I audited most of the courses which were being offered in the Spring quarter 1986. It was a new experience for me. The courses I decided to audit were mostly on non-Western music such as African, Middle Eastern and South-East Asian music. Under-graduate courses were divided into two 1½ hour classes per week or three 1 hour classes per week. Graduate seminars were held once a week for 3 hours. Class attendance varied from about 100–200 students in introductory courses to 10–20 in senior level courses. I sat with the students during class hours.

At the beginning of each course, hand-outs specially prepared for the subject were usually distributed to the students. These included topics to be covered, reading and listening assignments and description of audio tapes that went with the material. Lecturing was aided by films, slides and live performances by guest artists. Students were encouraged to participate either by singing, playing an instrument or joining in group dances. Senior students were often invited to introductory level classes to demonstrate. This gave them first hand experience of the actual music that they were studying. Often, to create proper cultural context, special drinks and foods such as Arabian coffee and snacks were offered in class as students or guest artists performed in traditional costumes. Questions-answers and discussions were a regular feature of all classes. The reading and listening assignments which were given to the students prepared the background for the next class. Students had to sign up their names in advance at a special listening laboratory in the music library to reserve a time to listen to the class tapes.

STUDENTS

Student life in the States is not easy. To be a student is a full time commitment specially at the graduate level. Most students have to support themselves at the university. They have to pay their fees, provide for books, room and boards. Some manage to get jobs on campus depending on their skills and interests; others manage to find grants and scholarships on the basis of their academic standing. I observed that teacher-student relation was quite informal. Students addressed their teachers by their first name, a practice I found a little uncomfortable. Another feature which I found strange was the way students conducted themselves especially in junior classes. They sat anyway they like, often with legs outstretched and drank or ate while the lecture was in process. The general atmosphere was very free. I found students curious, interested and open.

The academic year in North America is divided into four quarters—Fall, Winter, Spring, and Summer, or into three semesters—Fall, Winter, and Summer. In the first case, each quarter is of three months, in the second of four months. A full year course is usually three quarters or two semesters long. After each quarter or semester, and half-way in-between, students are given tests on the portions taught. The final marks are accumulative. This puts less strain on the student to remember the whole course for one final exam. Students are graded specially on the materials that have been covered in class lectures and reading lists. Since the syllabus of each teacher differs slightly depending on his special area, the students tend to attend classes regularly.

Graduate students often have appointments with their advisors to discuss their papers or theses. There is more one-to-one communication between student and teacher at this level and the faculty take keen interest in the research of their graduate students. This encourages students and also helps further explore areas that the faculty members themselves cannot because of work and other pressures. Graduate students with good academic standing are often made teaching assistants and they help the professor of the course in the preparation of course materials, exam and grading. This decreases the strain on teachers as well as gives good training to graduates.

The keen interest Westerners take in Indian music comes to the foreground especially in the research work of their graduate students and faculty. Right from the selection of a topic to the methods used to treat it and the final presentation, research in the West reflects a different attitude and training from the one in India. The source materials used for the basis of research and analysis are also vast and varied in comparison to what is used for similar studies in India.

FACULTY

Most of the faculty were Ph.Ds. In addition to their excellent academic backgrounds, they were also very good performers and some even continued to work on the professional platform. All members of the faculty are assessed on a yearly basis by both the students and their colleagues. There is constant pressure on faculty and they are expected besides teaching to increase their own knowledge, publish, participate at learned conferences and guide graduate theses. Along with formal course work, both faculty and students are expected to engage in extra-curricular activities on and off campus.

ACTIVITIES

An important feature of the Spring quarter was its well advertised concerts given by students, faculty and guest-artists and held at noon, in the evenings and during the week-ends in concert halls, in recital rooms or in the open fields. It was practically impossible to attend all these events, but they were a very important part of the students' activities and each recital given by a student marked an advancement of his skill and learning.

NORTH INDIAN CLASSICAL VOCAL MUSIC

In Indian music, UCLA offered one class in *sitaar* and one in *tablaa*. Since I was going to be there, I was requested to teach a course in North Indian classical vocal music. This was the first time UCLA offered such a course in North Indian classical vocal music. I had about fifteen students enrolled for this class. Most of them were Americans. Although they were music students, they had no background in Indian music, except for two students. I had to start them with the very basics, but they learnt to sit on the floor and sing well enough to present a ten minute item at the Ethnomusicology Spring Festival Concert.

The male students had very low, deep, broad and heavy voices and the females students had comparatively higher pitches. The students had good pick-up and in a few lessons could sing the various exercises, I taught them. They learnt *raag Kalyaan* and at the concert sang two of my compositions, one in medium tempo *Jhap taal* and another *taraanaa* in *drut Teentaal* which they enjoyed singing. Their pronunciation used to amuse me, but it takes a long time to be able to correctly pronounce words in a foreign tongue. Everything they sang—*aalaap, sargam, sargam-taan* was pre-composed by me and they memorised it. On the day of the concert, the girls wore *saree*-s and the boys *salwar khamiz*. They did very well. I also gave a concert on the same evening as a special guest. It was a great feeling.

The fellowship offered to me was only for three months—barely one quarter of the full year's teaching programme. However, I was very glad that I had the opportunity to study a new discipline in music. It has enriched my own knowledge and understanding of music of other cultures. I am convinced that with a background in Ethnomusicology and World music, a student of music will be able to see his own music in a new light and become more curious about the uniqueness of his own musical tradition. It will also equip him with the methods and outlook that are required to make a comparative study of different musical cultures including Indian music. In India itself, there are so many varieties of music, and by developing skills on how to study music in culture, a student will be able to analyse the diversity in music in India as well. He will also appreciate the need for interdisciplinary training. If students in India are equipped with proper background and training they will be able to come up with authoritative respectable research, especially because an Indian working on Indian music will give more authenticity to cultural context and feeling.

15

MUSIC CRITICISM: A PLEA FOR ARTIST-CRITIC UNDERSTANDING

Reviewing music in the print media today has become a powerful means of publicity. One can imagine therefore, what important and crucial role the critic plays in shaping public opinion about an artist and his art. As there are good performers and bad performers, there are good music critics and bad music critics. With due respect to our good music critics, I would like to mention a few things that I have observed as a performer, listener and teacher.

The art which takes form in solitude or that which exists only for the artist, is open to appreciation or criticism only by its creator. When another person happens to come into contact with this piece of art, he may react by accepting it or rejecting it. At times, he may even analyse his reactions consciously; but such reactions are often confined to himself and do not acquire any public value. When a critic steps into the world of art, his individual opinion, as that of a knowledgeable authority, is respected by all, even by those who have not experienced art themselves. The irony about the performing arts—music, dance and drama is that they exist only during the process of being performed and dissolve into nothingness thereafter making re-assessment impossible in the context of criticism made by the critic unlike painting, sculpture and literature which once created continue to exist unless destroyed. Recordings of music concerts, even if made, not only fail to capture the prevailing atmosphere/mood but also cannot possibly be circulated as widely due to a number of limitations, including the cost. Thus the writing of the reporter/music-critic becomes the only source of information of a concert and like a double-edged sword, it can either make or break the future of an artist. The background, education, practical experience, likes and dislikes and also vested interests of the critic naturally affect his judgement directly or indirectly; and whatever its worth in terms of accuracy, it is printed and sent out for wide publicity. Thus the majority of today's literate populace as well as the intelligentsia are media-fed in its idea about the performers and the performing arts.

Because of the special position which a critic enjoys, he gets a number of opportunities to express openly his views about the artist, the listeners and the organisers. The latter, however, seldom get an opportunity to say publicly what they feel about the critic and his criticism.

For many such reasons, music criticism has become a very sensitive and complicated subject. It needs to be studied as a whole discipline. Its present form, its positive and negative effects on art, artists and society, its future, all these aspects need to be studied carefully.

From times immemorial, man has felt the urge to delight and entertain his fellow men. In case of music, it assumed a concrete form popularly known today as the *mehfil*. One does not know when the artist-listener relationship came into existence. But, it also gave rise to the positions of organizer and critic.

The organizer, the artist, the listener and the critic are four pillars of *mehfil* today. They are responsible for the practical and aesthetic aspects of *mehfil* as an institution which includes organization, its customs and courtesies, creative process, psychological rapport and evaluation.

With the passage of time, the form and the content of *mehfil* have undergone manifold changes, making it more fascinating and technically more competent.

The *mehfil* is a unique institution. It is this institution that has preserved and assisted the evolution and development of Indian music. Without meaning to be such, it has become a 'workshop' that moulds the form, content and expression of Indian music.

The shaping spirit at work is a compound of the likes, dislikes and idiosyncrasies of both the artist and the listener. The form of today's Indian music is thus the outcome, mainly of the rapport and conflict, through centuries, between the artist and the listener.

Earlier, the organizer, the artist and the listener were the three constituents of the *mehfil*. The addition of a reviewer from the mass media has affected *mehfil* in a big way. A newspaper review is fast becoming an essential aspect of a *mehfil* and is assuming an increasing importance in the public life. It has, therefore, now become necessary to examine from time to time the interrelationship between these four constituents, and their mutual responsibilities and duties towards one another.

The practical aspects of a *mehfil* are:

1. Organization by the patron or organizer
2. The actual performance by the artist
3. Its appreciation by the listeners
4. The evaluation by a music critic

The organizer's activities begin before the *mehfil* proper. The artist and listeners are involved in the actual performance and appreciation. The critic, on the other hand begins to play his active role only after the *mehfil* is over.

The organizer, the artist and the listeners come in contact with one other for one reason or another and hence a degree of rapport between these constituents is established, but the critic tries to remain often either on the fringe of or even outside the *mehfil*. He behaves like a stranger with no desire to communicate or interact with the *mehfil*'s constituents. As between the artist and his listeners, it is equally necessary that there exists a rapport between the artist and the critic. Today such rapport is nowhere in sight. The absence of rapport or accord has caused a decline in the character of the criticism of performing arts

It cannot be debated that an artist who wins public recognition and continues to stay at the top, does so because he has stood the test of common and knowledgeable listeners' approval. He holds sway on the strength of his merit, which has received sanction and confirmation from the listeners. Paradoxically enough, a music critic who evaluates even a top ranking artist is supposed to need no specific qualifications, or undergo no competence test to qualify for his onerous task. In fact, every listener is a critic, he too evaluates; but his individual assessment does not appear in the newspaper columns. The critic's evaluation, on the other hand, is given wide publicity. He enjoys a privilege that is denied to the common listener. This implies that the critic, in so far as this privilege goes, is a person apart from all others. He should, therefore, be a person with more than ordinary competence and expertise, having a greater sense of responsibility in the discharge of his duties, and above all having integrity.

Art lovers who may not be present at a *mehfil*, experience music through the medium of the newspaper criticism. When such is the position, it is reasonable to expect that every word used by a critic should be weighed and carefully examined by him before being put into print. However, one is sorry to say that this expectation is rarely fulfilled by critics.

The *mehfil* may be 'just' a concert to others but for an artist it is the focus of an aspiration of his life, also the source of his livelihood. Every *mehfil* is a new test for him, an ordeal through which he and his art must pass.

The critic is often a more fortunate person. He never faces such a trial by fire. He can look upon his criticism as a 'side-business', 'a pastime', a 'hobby' or as an 'offshoot of his reporting work'. With such a casual attitude to music and its criticism, it is no wonder that criticism often sadly lacks high seriousness and depth.

Criticism is both an art and a science. It can be mastered only by those who are prepared to invest strenuous labour in it. For the artist, systematic training, sustained study and contemplation are regarded as basic requirements. Are they not equally indispensable for the music critic? Is a working knowledge of music and some writing skill enough to become a music critic? The art of music and its exposition has a tradition that goes back thousands of years. By contrast, newspaper criticism of music, particularly in India, is still in its infancy. It has yet to evolve an equally impressive tradition, its own conventions, discipline and language too. This is something that cannot be achieved overnight. It might take years, perhaps a generation or two. No wonder there is a strong demand by the artists, listeners and researchers to groom critics by special training.

Special training courses for music critics is the first right step in this direction. And only such academically oriented candidates should be absorbed by the press to give music criticism the much desired healthy turn. There is a great danger that the future scholar of music might look upon these reviews as source material for his research work. A review should be in simple language, employ definite musical terms wherever appropriate, and convey the musical activity/facts distinctly. Sensational headings, play on words, flowery language are gimmicks and should be avoided.

There are several reasons for the success or failure of a *mehfil*. If other constituents of a *mehfil* are indifferent or passive, the artist alone can do very little to make the *mehfil* a joyous experience. What do our music critics do in such cases? The general experience is that they sit in the front row with blank faces. They are unable to forget that they are music critics, that they are different from the listeners.

The artist, of course, has a natural stake in the *mehfil*, but the same cannot be said of a music critic. More often than not, he is engrossed in recording new and unfamiliar shocks to his own concept and knowledge of music. If this happens he may easily ignore the best that is presented by the artist and harp on what he subjectively thinks, ought to have been presented. He must remember that he is not free from the human weakness of personal preconceptions and limitations which can vitiate his judgement or estimate. It must be remembered that every *mehfil* need not and cannot be a success. The artist also knows this, but his minimum expectation is that the facts are accurately and objectively recorded and reported fairly without doing him injustice. Along with his individual assessment, the critic should also take into consideration the collective response of the listeners. He must have patience to let an artist grow in a concert or over a lifetime before pronouncing judgement. Each artist needs to be evaluated in terms of his assimilation of the tradition that has come down to him from previous generations, his interpretation of that tradition in the context of his contemporaries and his innovative and enduring contribution to tradition.

Condemning innovative artists at the very outset is blocking new paths of progress. Such an artist should be given sufficient time to grow in his endeavour towards the 'new'. Performing arts are 'live' creations. The human element present, makes them liable to ups and downs. In such cases, the critic needs to take a generous and sympathetic view and bring out the best in the creative attempt rather than stress incidental flaws.

Most concerts warm up after the interval. The warming-up process applies equally to the artist, listener and critic. Therefore, to listen to half a concert and express an opinion on it would be unfair to the artist. The evaluation should be of the whole, of the total. Analysing only one item would be unfair. The success of the concert depends on the active participation of all the constituents, as also on other related matters.

A gratifying concert of an upcoming artist and a concert by an established artist who has failed to come upto his standard should be projected differently. An awareness of the learning, the experience and the seniority of the artist should be clearly seen in the reviews. Reviewing certain artists and neglecting others amounts to giving publicity unfairly to a few. Even when there are several artists performing on the same day, a particular artist gets disproportionate attention. In some cases, even private concerts are covered, while public ones are ignored. There should be some criteria for the selection of the performance to be reviewed.

An artist has to strike a balance between his art and the demands of his profession. He has to reach his audience which today comprises people of varying tastes and demands. A critic must also take notice of the inevitable interplay between artist and audience.

Most important of all, a critic ought to make it a point to meet the artist immediately after the concert is over and get his point of view where there appears to be an occasion for unfavourable comment, say for choice of *raag*, its interpretation, etc. The artist's point of view should also be projected in the review.

Since it is the policy of the Government to promote the highly valued classical arts, it also becomes the responsibility of the newspapers to appoint qualified persons for reviewing the programmes. There should be definite norms, an ethical code to be followed by music critics.

Each newspaper, magazine should have at least two critics so that all the performances—even those held simultaneously are covered properly. Music reviews need to be presented artfully with photographs and for this sufficient space should be reserved on a specific day of the week. The publication of the reviews should not be by preference, it should follow the order of the events as they take place.

It has been observed that the critics generally work under poor conditions. This makes them vulnerable to special favours. Thus arise the hazards and the vices of working under obligations. The press would do better by improving working conditions of their staff and raising their remuneration to a standard befitting the dignity and gravity of their profession.

Classical music and musicians today are facing problems. The music critic must show a greater sense of responsibility and lighten their burden by sharing it. One solution could be frequent meetings, more dialogue between the artist and the critic. This will be a step towards a healthy relationship between the artist and the critic and a meaningful music criticism in general.

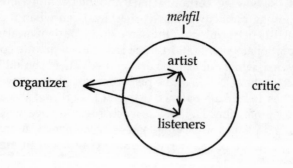

INDEX